AMBER

KALA JANAE

This book is a work of fiction. Names, characters, places, and incidentals either are products of the author's imagination or are used fictitiously. Any resemblance to actual events or locales or persons, living or dead, is entirely coincidental.

Copyright © 2019 Kala Janae
All rights reserved, including the rights to reproduction in whole or in part in any form.

DEDICATION

Dedicated to all the men and women who have survived a traumatic experience. Keep smiling and keep pushing forward on your road of healing. You are STRONGER than you believe!

ACKNOWLEDGMENTS

I have to start by thanking my friends and family. Each of you have been so inspirational and encouraging in my life. No matter how many times I wanted to give you, you kept pushing me forward. Thank you for listening to me gripe about how things weren't going the way I wanted them to and for allowing me to bounce ideas off you. Thank you for your prayers and for not giving up on me. This book is for you.

Alexis

1 THE SCARE

"Amber!" I looked at her limp body lying on the ground. "Amber! Amber wake up!!" I began shaking her 5'4 limp body lying on the ground. I quickly grabbed my cell phone and dialed 911. After the dispatcher told me that help was on the way, I went back to Amber to check on her again. I placed my fingers on her pulse and felt how feeble it was. Lord, please make them hurry and get here. I wondered what happened here.

    I had been calling Amber all day, but she never picked up the phone. It was so unlike her, so I decided to drop by and check on her. Luckily, she had given me a key to her apartment a few weeks ago, which made it quite easy to have access to her apartment. After knocking on the door a few times, I used my key to let myself in. As I walked in, everything seemed to be in order.

    I loved Amber's apartment. It was a 1400 sq. foot apartment decorated in a red, black, and white theme. Her sense of style was impeccable. She kept her apartment clean, neat, and clutter free. I wished I could be more like her.

    She was a damn good hairstylist here in Savannah, Georgia. She had one of the most successful hair salons in the area. Women would come from all around Georgia to get their hair done at Hairlicious Designs. As I walked into Amber's bedroom, I saw her lying on the floor surrounded by splattered pills. I immediately rushed toward her and started calling her name. After I didn't receive a response from her, I called 911.

    Amber McGee was my best friend. We met last year at the local

Jamaican festival. I had gone there alone due to being new to Savannah, Georgia. I moved here from Manning, SC and had only been here for only two weeks. I was tired of sitting in my apartment all alone, and so I figured what the hell.

When I got to the festival, it was so live. As I walked around looking at all the vendors, I came upon this one vendor selling Bob Marley paraphernalia. As I was looking at the bongs, posters and Bob Marley shirts, I felt a presence next to me. I looked over and saw the most beautiful female I had ever seen. She was about 5'4, caramel complexion, with golden brown natural wavy hair. She was dressed in a long olive-green sundress with a golden belt tied around her waist.

She saw me looking at her and she smiled, "Hello, I'm Amber."

I reciprocated as I reached out my hand and shook hers, "I'm Alexis. Nice to meet you Amber." I said.

She looked around to see if I was with anyone. When she noticed that no one was tagging along with me she said, "Are you here by yourself?"

I was too embarrassed to admit that I was, and so I softly said, "Yes, I am."

She smiled brighter and said, "So am I. Would you like us to enjoy the festival together?"

In my head, I shouted of course I would, I hope we hit it off. Then, verbally I said, "Sure, why not. Let's give it a shot." We ended up hitting it off big time; and found out we had so much in common. Before we left the festival that night, we exchanged numbers and promised to call each other the next day.

There was finally a knock on the door with a yell for 911. I quickly ran to the door and let them in. "She's in the bedroom unconscious. Down the hall, first room on the left. Please, help her!" I said frantically.

"Ma'am, we'll do everything possible to help your friend." This 6-foot-tall Hispanic paramedic said, and they quickly went in the room. It might have just been my nerves, but it felt like they had her on that stretcher in a matter of seconds. As they pushed the gurney out of the house and placed her in the ambulance, they told me to follow them to the hospital.

I hopped in my car and was ready to go in a split second. Luckily, the hospital was only ten minutes away from Amber's house. On the drive to the hospital, I kept trying to figure out why Amber would do something like this to herself. She seemed so happy. She had been distant for the past few weeks, but I figured that was because she was busy at work. I snapped out of my thoughts and decided to focus on the drive to the hospital and finding a parking spot before both of us ended up in the hospital.

When I pulled up to the hospital, I saw someone pulling out that had front row parking. I quickly pulled in and ran toward the hospital doors. As I rushed through the front door, everyone turned to see what was going on. It didn't pay any attention to those nosey people, instead I just went straight to the front desk and waited in line. After ten minutes of standing there waiting, my patience was shot by the time I reached the front counter. I had to close my eyes and take a deep breath before I lost my cool.

"Excuse me ma'am, the ambulance just brought my friend, Amber McGee, in. I'm her best friend and I found her in her apartment. I am the one who called 911." I said in a calm tone.

This skinny, pale, blond haired nurse looked at me and said in an annoying voice, "Please, fill out this information for her and I will keep you posted. Does she have any immediate family in the area that you would like to call?"

I took a deep breath to calm my anger and said, "No ma'am, I'm the closest thing that she has as a relative." I quickly took the paperwork from her and filled it out to the best of my knowledge. After I gave the nurse the paperwork back, I sat down in a chair in the corner and began to pray for her.

"Heavenly Father, I come to you now in prayer to lift Amber up to you. I don't know what she was going through that made her attempt to take her life Lord. Lord, please help take the pain away from her. Please Lord! Please, help her to pull through this and to heal her sick mind, Lord. Amber has been very faithful to you, Lord. She just had a weak moment and stumbled. Please, hear my prayer Lord. In Jesus name I pray, Amen."

Just as the 'Amen' left my mouth, I heard a deep baritone voice say, "Mrs. White?" I was not prepared for what my eyes would behold when I opened them.

When I opened my eyes, I saw this fine ass bald headed doctor staring down at me. He was 5'9, deep brown eyes, these sexy sensual pink lips, sun kissed brown skin, and he had the nerve to have dimples on his cheeks. I was so taken aback that I was rendered speechless.

"Mrs. White? Are you Mrs. White?" he repeated. I just sat there staring at this wonderful creation that God made. "Ma'am, are you alright? "He asked looking at me a little closer."

Snap out of it, Alexis. Amber needs you right now, I told myself. I finally got my legs to work and stood up. "Yes, I'm sorry about that doctor. I'm Ms. White. Is Amber doing alright?" I managed to say.

"If you're sure you're alright, will you please follow me?" he said. He quickly turned around and began walking down the hallway.

As I followed him, I watched the way his body moved in the white doctors coat he had on.

"Ms. White?" Did you hear me?" the fine doctor said.

I was so lost daydreaming about his body that I didn't notice that he stopped walking and was facing me. "I'm sorry doctor... What's your name?" I said apologetically.

He looked at me and shook his head, "That's what I just told you. My name is Doctor Daniel Bradshaw. I'm the one who just pumped all that oxycodone out of your friend, Amber. I came to tell you that she is alive and that she is asleep right now. She should be awake in a few minutes. Do you know why she would try to commit suicide?" He stated in a concerned voice.

As a tear escaped my eyes, I said, "No. She was making a lot of changes at her business since she just opened it up a one year ago. We hadn't talked in a few weeks, so I figured maybe it was because of everything that was going on at Hairlicious Designs. I was worried about her, so I showed up to her house to check on her. Luckily, she had given me a house key two weeks before. I'm sorry I couldn't be of more assistance to you." I said sadly. "What is the next course of action?"

He looked at the tears flowing from my eyes and said, "She will have to be on suicide watch for the next 72 hours. We will keep her here, monitor her, and make sure she doesn't try to harm herself again. We will keep her under close observation, and you are welcome to stay as long as you want with her. I have other patients to tend to now. Push the button on the bed if
you or Amber need anything." He said as he turned away to walk out the door.

My stomach was tied in a knot, but I would not be able to get over this if I didn't ask. "Excuse me doctor Bradshaw?" I said as I watched this magnificent specimen of a man turn back around and look at me.

"Yes Ms. White," he said as those beautiful eyes stared deep into my soul.

"This may be so inappropriate, but you are so damn fine." I said softly.

No, those words did not just leave my mouth. I could be so awkward at times.

Those dimples appeared as he smiled, "Why thank you. I think you are damn sexy yourself. Here's my card if you ever want to talk." He turned and walked away.

I can't believe that pick up line just worked on him. I looked at his cream-colored business card with his information boldly engraved on it in gold letters. Damn, I thought to myself, this man is fine and has style. As I switched my focus back to Amber, I went and sat by her bedside.

I clasped her left hand in mines and just sat looking at her. I just can't figure out why she would try to kill herself. She didn't mention having any problems in life and she seemed relatively happy. That just goes to show you how people can put on a happy appearance on the outside and be downright depressed on the inside.

As I sat there lost in thought, I heard a small feeble voice say, "Alexis?"

I quickly snapped out of my thoughts and said, "Amber, you're alright! I'm here for you girl. Are you alright?"

She looked at me with the saddest expression on her face, "Yes, I'm alright. I'm sorry for putting you through this."

As the tears flowed down my face, I asked her, "Why did you do it? Why didn't you come to me, I would have tried to help you get through whatever it was you were going through? I'm your friend, I will always be here for you." I said in between sobs.

She pushed the button by her beside as she watched the tears flow down my face, "I'm sorry Alexis. After I get this glass of water, I will start from the beginning and tell you everything."

We sat there staring at each other until the nurse came in. Once the nurse brought in the two glasses of water that Amber requested, she asked the nurse to close the door. As the door closed, she started talking in this voice that I had never heard before. It was filled with so much pain and anger.

AMBER'S STORY

2 FACADES

I was born in a small town on the outskirts of Memphis, Tennessee. When I was fifteen years old, my mother, Laura, became strung out on drugs. Whatever drug you can name, she was on it. I had never seen someone as high as my mother was. Not a day went by that she wasn't strung out on some type of drugs. It was so bad that my father, John, couldn't take it anymore. He tried numerous times to convince her to get help, but she blatantly refused. It got to the point where my father became an alcoholic, and things became more complicated. I remember it like it was yesterday.

One night when I was seventeen years old, my father stumbled home from the bar. I was in my bed sleeping when I heard what sounded like furniture being knocked over. I quietly ran to the top of the stairs and peered over the banister. My mom and dad were standing in the foyer; I could hear my mom pleading for my daddy to be quiet before he woke me up. Instead, my daddy turned into a raging monster.

"Don't you tell me what to do you little slut. I know all about your hoeing tendencies. I went to the bar down on Jackson Street and when I walked in, everyone began laughing. I didn't know what they were laughing at, and so I just sat down at the bar and tried to let it go.

Once I had a few drinks, I just couldn't get it off my mind. I asked the bartender what everyone was laughing at when I walked in. He looked at me and told me he thinks I should go home. I declined and insisted that he tell me what it was all about.

After asking him a few more times, he told me something that was not so damn funny." Daddy looked at my mother and said, "Do you have anything to say Laura?"

She just stood there looking back at him while shaking her head to signal a no.

"Yes, you do bitch, don't lie to me! He told me that you were fucking various men around town to get money for your drug habit. Are you going to deny it, Laura?"

My mother responded in the calmest voice that I had ever heard her use, "Yes John, it's true. I've started going to the doctor to get help. He says that I have a drug addiction problem and that he could help me fix it. I'm trying to..."

Before my mother could finish her sentence, my father had picked up the metal statue by the door and brought it down between my mother's eyes. The next thing I know, my mother was laid out on the floor with a stream of blood coming out of her head. For a split second, I stared frozen in horror at the scene in front of me. I quickly ran down the hall and called 911. By the time the police had arrived, my father had split both of his wrists in the kitchen.

I took a pause from my story to see how Alexis was handling it. When I looked over at her, she was on the edge of her seat with her mouth wide open. Once she saw me looking at her, she closed her mouth and said, "Oh my goodness, Amber. I am so sorry you had to endure that at such an early age".

I frowned at her, "I'm not finished yet. Are you sure you want me to continue?" She looked at me like she wasn't sure. Then, she silently shook her head to signal a yes. So, I continued unleashing my demons upon her.

After the police came, they took me in to child protective service. Following the long drawn out process, they determined that I only had one living relative; my uncle Samuel living down in Long Beach, Mississippi. They helped me pack up all my belongings and a worker drove me to my Uncle Samuel's house.

As we drove into Long Beach, it didn't seem too bad. From the looks of it, it seemed to be a beautiful community. It was about 7:00 am when we drove in, so the town was bustling with students going to school. As we drove by the high school, I figured that it was the one that I would be attending. Long Beach High School was a nice-looking school.

Ten minutes later, we drove up a winding driveway and parked in front of a two-story red brick house. It had a wraparound porch, huge bay windows, and sun stained patio furniture. The yard looked to be about two acres and looked to be months overdue for yard care. There were two vehicles in the yard. One was a run-down rusted red Chevy truck and the other vehicle looked to be a shiny white Chevy Impala.

As I stared at the scene before me, I didn't get a good vibe from the place. I was startled out of my thoughts by the social worker who slammed the car door shut. I slowly pulled myself out of the car and grabbed my bags.

As I placed my bags down on the porch, I reached my hand up to knock on the door. Before I could knock, the door swung open. A tall fit man stood before me. He was about 5'9 and the color of melted dark chocolate. Uncle Samuel had a fresh fade, mahogany brown eyes, and had a freshly trimmed goatee. He was wearing a navy-blue suit with a cream-colored tie, and black suede shoes. No woman could deny that he was a handsome man.

On the ride here, the social worker had told me a little about Uncle Samuel. He was a well-respected gynecologist at the only hospital in town. Uncle Samuel graduated at the top of his class at Morehouse College and moved to Long Beach to start life anew.

When he saw me standing right in front of him, he smiled and said, "Hello Amber, welcome to your new home!" I just stood there staring at him. I couldn't get over the fact that he resembled Mama so much. He looked like her identical twin, but the male version of her. How could they expect me to live with someone who looked exactly like my dead mother? I would see her deceased face every time I looked at him.

He saw the look on my face and said, "Yes, your mother and I look exactly alike. The funny thing is we weren't even twins. I'm sorry for your loss by the way. Your mother was a great woman; I wish we would have gotten to spend more time together." When he said that last sentence, this eerie smile came across his face. He quickly snapped out of whatever thought he was having and told us to come in. My first impression of him was that he was a nice man, but something about him was off.

As all three of us dragged my bags into the house, I was amazed by what I saw. Although the outside of his house was lacking in some areas, the inside of his house was immaculate. As I walked through the door, it opened to a marble foyer decorated in a rich gold Egyptian theme. The first door that we came to on the right side opened to a beautiful living room decorated in a soft cream and gold. My jaw dropped as I turned to look at him. "This is your home?" I said. "You live here by yourself?"

He gave out that creepy smile again and said, "No, you and I live here now. Place your bags right here, I will get you situated in your room once I sign all your paperwork. Please, take a look around the place."

Without hesitation, I quickly obliged. I left the living room and walked down the hall to what appeared to be the kitchen and the dining room. Both areas were huge and elegantly decorated. As I went up the stairs, there were four more rooms. I went to the one to the right of the stairs in the corner. I opened the door and my mouth dropped open. There was no way this could be my room, it was perfect.

The walls were painted a soft lilac purple with lilacs stenciled on the wall. There was a huge cherry red queen canopy bed in the center of the back wall, along with two matching dressers and a vanity mirror. There was a large cream-colored rug on the floor with my name embroidered on it along with a lilac flower. To the right of the door leading into the room was another door. I opened the door and turned the light on; I could barely believe my eyes on the sight I had to behold. There was a huge Jacuzzi tub, a walk-in shower, and the bathroom was decorated in an elephant theme. How did he know I loved elephants?

As I stepped out the bathroom, I noticed double doors directly across the room. I walked across the room and slowly opened the doors. All I could do was stand there dumbfounded. It was a gigantic walk in closet with rows and rows of clothes and shoes. Each part of the closet was categorized by like items. I walked into the closet and checked some of the sizes from each category, and they were all my sizes. How did he know my sizes, my favorite color, favorite flower, and my favorite animal? I didn't even know this man existed until two days ago. This was definitely creepy.

As I stood there staring in disbelief, I felt something on my arm. I quickly pulled my arm away as I looked to see what it was. It was Uncle Samuel. I was so lost in the creepiness that I didn't hear him walk in.

"It's alright Amber," he said. "It's just me, Uncle Samuel. You don't have to be afraid."

As I stared at him dumbfounded, I said, "Why did you decorate my room like this and how did you know what sizes I wore?"

He let out that eerie smile again and responded, "You don't like it? I think it's beautiful."

My intentions were not to be rude, so I responded, "Yes, I love it, it's absolutely gorgeous. I was just wondering how you knew what I liked?"

He looked at me thoughtfully as if he was trying to determine what to say. "Oh, I'm glad you like it. Your birthday is coming up in a few months, isn't it? Your mother was telling me that she wanted to redo your room and your bathroom, so I decided to make that wish come true for her. You've been traveling for hours, so why don't you wash up and get ready for dinner. Come down to the kitchen when you finish." He turned and walked out the door. "Oh, I like to dress formal for dinner, so you should wear one of those dresses in your closet."

I went into the bathroom and started filling the tub with warm water. Something told me to look under the bathroom sink to see if there was any bubble bath. When I looked inside, I was amazed to see that there were rows of bubble bath, bath bombs, and various scented soaps for me to use as well. Uncle Samuel had really hooked me up. I was not use to this type of lifestyle and treatment. I grew up so poor back in Memphis. After the water finished running, I soaked myself in the tub. I couldn't believe the sequence of events that had led to me being here.

How could Papa kill mama then commit suicide? Why didn't he think about me before he made those decisions? Why would he do this to me? Didn't he love me? How would my life be living here with Uncle Samuel in Long Beach, Mississippi? Would I be treated like an outcast since I was new to the school? I'm only seventeen years old. How would I be able to deal with this new chapter in my life?

After twenty minutes of crying in the tub, I heard Uncle Samuel yell that dinner was ready. As I got out the tub, I enjoyed the warmth that the towel gave me. I would never feel the warm embrace of mama or daddy again.

I walked to my new closet and went to the dress section. There were so many dresses to choose from; summer dresses, church dresses, exquisite dresses, and dresses to wear around the house. I settled on a dark navy-blue church dress with the matching flats.

After getting dressed, I sat at the vanity mirror and brushed my hair back into a bun. After checking out myself in the mirror, I started my decent down the stairs. As I got closer to the bottom of the stairs, I heard classical music plating in the background from the dining room area.

Classical music like mama use to listen to when she cooked dinner. Uncle Samuel and mama were definitely related because not a lot of black people listened to classical music. Upon entering the kitchen, I saw Uncle Samuel sitting at the head of the table. Once he saw me enter, he stood up, walked around the table and pulled my chair out. I sat down and he pushed my chair up to the table.

Would he do this every time we had dinner? Did he really expect me to dress up every night? As I looked at the spread on the table, I could not believe that there was so much food. He had made spaghetti with two types of garlic bread, a fresh salad, turkey chops, apple pie, fresh squeezed lemonade, a pitcher of tea, and sweet potato pie. "Why did you make so much food Uncle Samuel?" I said really feeling concerned. This was too much.

Uncle Samuel laughed and said, "This is the normal spread that I make for dinner. I like options. Please, help yourself to any of these."

I was starving so I was not about to play any games with this food. There was a plate in front of me, and so I picked it up and fixed me some of everything except for the dessert. Mama always made me get my dessert after I finished eating all of my food.

As I quickly ate my food, I noticed that Uncle Samuel was staring at me and hadn't touched his food yet. After swallowing the mouth full of food, I stated, "Sorry Uncle Samuel, I'm starving. We had some nasty McDonalds on the way here. It was burnt and I could barely eat it. Trust me, I don't normally eat like this."

He chuckled and said, "You're fine Amber. It's okay, and I know you're hungry. How was the drive down here?"

I took a pause to think and then said, "Honestly, I slept through most of the trip. I really enjoyed driving through Georgia though. It was very scenic out there. The most exciting part to me was being on and seeing a bridge for the first time."

He sat back and laughed hardily, "The bridge was the most exciting part? Wow! Now, that is something else. On a more sobering note, how are you handling the death of your parents?"

The plate rattled as my fork fell from my shaking hands and hit it. I quickly picked it up and regained my posture. "Sorry about that Uncle Samuel. For the most part, I think I'm handling the death of mama and papa pretty well. It's still hard to believe that they are gone though. It all seems like just yesterday I was sitting beside mama telling her how my day was. Unfortunately, I witnessed the whole incident. Papa came in drunk, he argued with mama, then he struck her between the eyes with a metal statue from the hallway. By the time I came back from calling 911, papa had killed himself too. I honestly just don't want to think about or talk about it. Hopefully, you can understand that Uncle Samuel."

He finally took a bite of his dinner. He slowly chewed his food as he sat there in deep thought. After each bite that he took, he put his fork down and whipped his mouth with his napkin. Wow, I thought to myself, he's so proper.

Finally, after a long awkward silence, he spoke to me again. "Amber, I can only imagine the grief and pain that you are feeling right now. Your mother and I were very close while growing up and basically up to the point until you were two years old. Your mother and I had a disagreement and she stopped talking to me for the following fourteen years. You don't know how glad I was when your mother reached out to me after fourteen years of shutting me out. With that being said, I loved your mom unconditionally. She was my family too, and it tore me apart when I got that phone call that she was dead. Please don't hesitate to come to me if you ever need anything, have any questions, or even want to rant about something. Not only am I your legal guardian, but I'm your friend as well. I want us to have an open line of communication; so, do not ever feel like you can't come to me with a problem or concern. I enjoyed this dinner. Get some sleep, we have to get you registered in school tomorrow."

As I stood up to go to my new room, I asked him, "Do you need help with the dishes?" Mama always made me help with the dishes after dinner.

He chuckled and said, "Laura raised you well. You can start helping with the dishes next week. Have a good night."

Laura, he called her Laura. Would he keep bringing up my dead mother? "Good night Uncle Samuel. I'll be ready to go at 7:00 am." He nodded his head in agreement.

The next day went by in such a blur. When I woke up that morning, Uncle Samuel had made a spread of pancakes, waffles, blueberry muffins, scrambled eggs, bacon, ham, and fresh squeezed orange juice. After breakfast, I ran upstairs and got dressed. I decided to wear a lace cream-colored three-quarter sleeve shirt, and a knee length black skirt. I paired that with some cream flats that I found in the closet, straightened my shoulder length black hair, and placed a black bow on the right side of my head. The school was 10 minutes away from Uncle Samuel's house.

When we got to the front office, the principal was already standing there waiting for us. She was a short, petite woman with blond hair. Her skin color reminded me of freshly stirred whitewash she could have used a tan. Once we walked up, she extended her hands to Uncle Samuel and began batting her eyelashes and talking in this southern drawl. Her name was Ms. Higgins and I could tell that she and I would not get along. She was so smitten over Uncle Samuel that she didn't even pay any attention to me. Finally, Uncle Samuel looked at me and stated, "This is Amber McGee, my niece. As you know, I am here to enroll her in your school."

Ms. Higgins placed a fake smile on her face as she turned toward me and said, "Why yes, of course. Amber McGee. Your old school sent me over your school record, and we were able to place you in the appropriate classes." After that brief introduction, she escorted us to her office and went over all my paperwork and her expectations from me. "Here is your schedule, I will have Monique come and show you around." From that moment forward, my day became a blur of new people and names.

By the time I got home at the end of the day, I was exhausted. I took off my school clothes, hung them up neatly and took a nap. When I awoke from my nap, it was 8:00 pm. I had slept for 4 hours straight, which means I really must have been tired. Dinner was at 7:00 pm, so I quickly rushed downstairs to see if Uncle Samuel was still there.

As soon as I made it to the bottom of the stairs, I heard Uncle Samuel yell, "Sleeping beauty has risen. How was your nap?" I ran into the living room where I saw him sitting reading the newspaper.

"Oh, Uncle Samuel, I'm so sorry I overslept and missed dinner. I didn't realize how tired I was." I gushed.

"It's alright princess. It was your first day of school after so many things have transpired in your life. I placed your plate in the microwave for you." He said kindly.

That was sweet of him I thought to myself. "Thank you, Uncle Samuel. You're so kind. I haven't told you this yet but thank you for taking me in to your beautiful home. This really does mean a lot to me," I said as I opened the microwave to see what he had cooked.

Inside was meat loaf, pork chops, garlic rolls, macaroni and cheese, and baked beans. Beside the microwave was a big bowl of freshly made salad. This meal looked delicious. I love how he always gave me options. A part of me felt bad though, because he always made so much food.

Uncle Samuel said, "You're welcome Amber. I would do anything for you darling. You're family. If the roles were switched, I would hope you would do the same for me as well."

I thought about it for a moment. If I had a niece or nephew whose parents died, would I take them in? That is a lot of responsibility, especially if you are already struggling to make ends meet. You know what, I would take them in. Uncle Samuel was right, we are family.

"Uncle Samuel, why do you always make so much food? What do you do with the leftovers? I noticed we haven't had leftovers yet."

Uncle Samuel let out a bellowing laugh as he said, "You're very observant Amber. I don't eat leftovers. Growing up, your Grandma, Camille, always made your mama and I eat leftovers, and I hated it. I told myself that once I got older, I would never eat leftovers again. I cook so much food because I enjoy giving to the needy. Every night before I go to bed, I divide the leftovers in containers and take them down to Sawgrass Park to the homeless people who frequent there. The next day I pick up the containers when I give them a new meal. Don't tell anyone though. The park closes at 5:30 pm and no one is supposed to be there."

I looked at him in admiration. Wow, he seemed like a really nice guy. That is such a noble thing to do. If only I could get over that creepy feeling he gives me though.

"Uncle Samuel, that's a remarkable thing to do. I know they appreciate you so much. Don't worry, your secret is safe with me. I would love to go with you on the weekends." I said.

"That would be great. I'm about to go upstairs for the night so you have a good night. Oh yeah, I will start back at work tomorrow, so you will have to take the bus from here on out. The bus will pick you up in front the house at 6:45 am."

The bus? Mama always took me to school; this was about to be a new experience. After I finished eating, I went up to my room and went to sleep.

Life was going good at Uncle Samuel's. I had made a few friends within the first three months that I had been there. One night as I was asleep in bed, this eerie feeling came over me and I awoke with a start. As I ground the sleep out of my eyes, I tried looking around the room as my eyes adjusted to the darkness. As I was scanning the room, I looked toward the door and noticed a man's silhouette. "Uncle Samuel?" I said with fear in my voice. As soon as I said that, he backed out of the doorframe and disappeared. I quickly jumped up out of my bed and ran to close and lock the door.

Mentally, I made a note to keep my door locked. As I crawled back into the bed, I laid there trying to figure out what had just happened. Why was Uncle Samuel standing in my door watching me sleep? I had to ask him when he got home for work. I looked at the clock and it was 1:00 am. No matter how hard I tried to go back to sleep, it eluded me.

After school, I rushed into the house, took off my school clothes, and finished my homework all before Uncle Samuel pulled into the driveway. When I heard his car pull up, I immediately ran to the door and waited for him in the foyer. He was talking on his cellphone when he came through the door, so I stood by waiting patiently for him to finish. He was so engrossed in his conversation that he walked right past me. Uncle

Samuel finally said goodbye and hung up the phone.

"Hello Uncle Samuel, how are you?" I asked him hesitantly, not really sure how I was going to have the courage to ask him.

"Oh, hi Amber, I didn't even see you standing right there. My boss was talking to me about one of my patients. I'm doing well, you?" he said sounding stressed out.

Was now the right time? I thought to myself. Let me just get this off my chest before it starts to consume me.

"Uncle Samuel?" I said as my voice lowered an octave.

He looked at me worried, "Is everything alright Amber? What happened?"

Damn it, I had him on edge now. "Why were you in my room last night at 1:00 am Uncle Samuel?" I quickly blurted out.

A look of confusion came over his face as he said, "What are you talking about Amber? I was not in your room at 1:00 am. I was sleeping." He stared at me waiting for an explanation.

"I saw you standing at my door Uncle Samuel. Please, just tell me what you were doing there?"

Anger quickly replaced the confusion that was written on his face.

He raised his voice at me in that firm parenting voice, "Amber, I don't appreciate you lying on me. I just told you that I was in my bed asleep at 1:00 in the morning. What the hell would I be doing in your room during that timeframe? I will not tolerate lying or disrespect in my house! This discussion is over! Sounds like you just had a bad dream." He then turned and walked up the stairs to his room.

Was I dreaming or did I really see Uncle Samuel in my room last night? As I replayed last night in my mind, I knew and was very sure I wasn't dreaming. It did happen, he was hiding something. I went upstairs to pass time until dinner was ready. At 7:00 pm I was dressed and ready for dinner. As I descended the stairs, I didn't smell any aromas coming from the kitchen, and I didn't even hear the classical music that normally played either.

When I got to the dining room, I was amazed to find that Uncle Samuel was not there and that there wasn't any food on the table. This was so unlike him. My first instinct was to go knock on his door to make sure he was alright.

As I climbed the stairs, I tried to remember the particular room that was his. I didn't get a chance to explore the other three bedrooms yet since the doors were always closed. As I thought back, I remembered seeing him coming out from the farthest room to the left of the top of the stairs. I rendered three loud knocks on the door and waited for an invitation to come in or an acknowledgement of my presence. I counted to twenty and knocked a little louder when I didn't get a response. Twenty more seconds went by and I knocked even louder, still no response.

That's odd, I thought to myself. He should be here because I didn't hear him leave. Turning around, I headed back downstairs to see if his cars were out front. Both Chevys' were parked outside, and I was convinced he was home. That's alright, I thought to myself. I will just fix me a sandwich and eat in my room. Maybe he overslept or didn't feel well. After I devoured my turkey and swiss cheese sandwich on multigrain bread, I returned downstairs to wash and dry my plate. Afterwards, I returned to my room and decided to call it a night.

I quickly awoke from my sleep when I felt that eerie feeling again. As I ground the sleep from my eyes, I automatically turned my eyes toward the door. The door was closed, so why did I have that feeling? As I began scanning the room, I jumped when my head turned to the left of the room. There was Uncle Samuel sitting in a chair in the corner of my room naked from head to toe. "Uncle Samuel, I yelled frantically! What are you doing in my room?"

Something told me that he didn't hear me. He slowly stood up, grabbed the kitchen chair, walked out of the room, and closed the door behind him. I jumped out the bed, ran over to the door, and locked it. Certainly tomorrow night, I wouldn't forget to lock my bedroom door. Once again, I had another sleepless night.

The next day, I didn't know if I should bring it up to Uncle Samuel or not. He was so angry yesterday after I confronted him. After Uncle Samuel got home from work and changed, I went to knock on his bedroom door. "Come in!" I heard him yell from the other side of the door. When I turned the knob and pushed the door open, I was not ready for the blasphemous view that I saw.

Uncle Samuel's room was huge, and much bigger than mine. Walking into his room, the first thing I saw was this huge portrait of Uncle Samuel naked holding his arms out in a welcome gesture. Underneath that was a large four poster oak king bed decorated in a black and red comforter. As I walked in farther, I turned my head to the left and saw that his bathroom was on that side of the room. He had a large oversize sofa and TV set up in the corner. To the right of his bed were two large black dressers in what appeared to be oak. Above the dressers was this large painting of this beautiful black woman who had her hair fanned about her face. She was naked in this painting and you could see every detail of her body. From this distance, something looked familiar about her.

The portrait was so mesmerizing that I slowly walked toward it to get a better view and wanting to soak it all up. When I stepped directly in front of the portrait, this involuntary loud scream left my mouth. I quickly turned and looked directly at Uncle Samuel. I was short of words as I just pointed back at the portrait. Uncle Samuel was just sitting back on his bed watching my every move. He kept his eyes on me as he said, "Yes, that's your mother. Isn't it such a beautiful painting?"

What kind of question is that, I thought to myself? Finally, I felt as if I was capable of forming words again. "Why do you have such a detailed naked picture of my mother, your sister, in your bedroom?" I shouted. That same look of confusion spread across his face, the same way it did yesterday when I confronted him.

"What do you mean why do I have the painting, Amber? It's a beautiful work of art that one of your mothers' ex-boyfriends painted of her. She once told me about the painting, and I knew that I had to have it. I didn't want anyone else having that piece hanging in their house. So, I bought it and hung it up. It was the most appropriate place in the house to place it." I was so dumbfounded that I didn't even know what to say. I just stared at him for what seemed like eternity.

Finally, I said, "Uncle Samuel, this is so inappropriate. That is a picture of your naked dead sister hanging in your bedroom. How do you think that's okay?"

He quickly jumped off his bed and started screaming at the top of his lungs, "Get the hell out of my room, Amber! You don't know anything about art! This picture of your mother, my sister is a masterpiece! This is my house; I can decorate it as I please! Go to your room and don't come out until it's time for you to go to school in the morning!"

I turned and started walking out of the room, just as I made it to the door, I said, "Uncle Samuel?"

Before I could even finish my sentence, he yelled, "Get the fuck out of my room Amber! Do as I say!"

Defeated, I walked away and stayed in my room for the remainder of the night. Before I laid down to sleep that night, I made sure to lock the door. Around 2:00 am I awoke to the sound of my door being shaken. I knew it was Uncle Samuel. Luckily, he gave up once he realized that he wasn't going to be able to open up the door. He will probably be even more upside tomorrow, but oh well, he's creepy as fuck.

For the next two weeks, things were back to normal in the house. Uncle Samuel didn't stop by my room anymore at night, and I never went in his room again. One particular day, I got home from school and went up to my room. As I approached my bedroom, I stopped dead in my tracks.

Every morning before I left for school, I straightened up my room and made sure that I closed the door. Not only could I see inside my bedroom from the hallway, but my entire door was gone. This crazy man really had my bedroom door removed. I was so livid that I stormed into my room, threw myself on my bed, and let the tears flow.

Why was he doing this to me? What had I done that was so bad that he had to invade my privacy and remove my bedroom door? Who removes bedroom doors as a punishment? Better yet, why am I even getting punished? I thought him and I were on semi good terms.

I cried so much that I cried myself to sleep. Two hours later, I awoke to Uncle Samuel calling my name. As I awoke fully, I just glared at Uncle Samuel.

"Are you alright Amber? I'm not use to you being asleep when I get home. Why were you crying?" he asked me in a genuinely concerned tone.

Without answering his questions, I flat-out asked him, "Where is my door, Uncle Samuel? Why did you remove it?"

The rage that came across his face was instantaneous. Without missing a beat, he crossed the room, and slapped the taste out of my mouth. I could feel the blood fly from my mouth as my face whipped around. "

Don't you ever question me again, Amber. I am the adult here, and this is my fucking house." He said angrily.

Before I could even respond, he turned and left my room. I could not believe that he had slapped me. My mama always told me that a real man would never abuse a woman. Uncle Samuel was just like daddy. I laid in my bed and cried myself to sleep again.

.

3 BROKEN CHAINS

When I awoke in the morning, the sun was shining down on my face. It was finally the weekend and I didn't have to go to school today. My goal for the day was to avoid Uncle Samuel at all cost. I'd concluded that he wasn't all the way there mentally. The confusion that came across his face every time I brought up him being in my room was scary. If I didn't know any better, I would believe him when he said he didn't do those things. He had to have some bipolar or multiple personalities issues going on within him. I'm not sure how long I would be able to tolerate his behavior.

    What I really wanted to know was how long it would be before he put my door back on the hinge. Uncle Samuel had really changed over the past few months. I honestly believe he had multiple personalities because a sane person would not behave this way. He went from being a sweet loving uncle to this mean psychotic bipolar man. I wondered how he was able to manage his patients at the clinic. After the whole artwork incident in his room, he stopped cooking dinner. I guess the homeless people in the park weren't that important anymore.

    I went down to the kitchen to fix me some breakfast; I really wanted some pancakes and eggs. When I walked into the kitchen, I was literally left speechless. This crazy man had placed locks on all of the cabinets and even on the refrigerator. How the hell was I supposed to eat?

    Without thinking, I quickly ran back upstairs and began banging on his bedroom door. "Uncle Samuel? Uncle Samuel?" I stood there waiting for him to acknowledge my presence at the door but there was no response. It was 9:00 am, so I know he was awake. "Uncle Samuel?" I called again a little louder.

    I placed my ear to the door and listened for any noises coming from the room. After two minutes of standing still, I didn't hear anything. I looked out of the window and noticed that one of his vehicles were gone. How could he lock up all the food and leave me here all by myself?

I tried calling him on his cellphone, but he didn't answer. Defeated, I walked back to my room and tried to go to sleep. Two hours later, I awoke with a growling stomach. I looked out the window to see if Uncle Samuel had made it home, but he hadn't. What was I going to do? I didn't have any money to walk to the convenience store that was 10 minutes away by foot.

I decided to search around the house to see if I could come up with any loose change. After about an hour of thorough searching, I had only found twenty-five cents. That wasn't going to buy me anything. Finally, I retreated to my room and decided to just write in my diary.

Three hours later, I heard the alarm on Uncle Samuels's car. I hopped out of the bed and flew down the stairs. As soon as he opened the door, he looked at me and kept walking without a word to me. How rude, I thought to myself.

"Uncle Samuel?" I said quietly.

He turned back, looked at me and said, "What do you want, Amber? Take your dramatic ass on somewhere." I was so taken aback that I couldn't even think of any words to say.

After a few seconds of standing there with my mouth wide open, I said, "Uncle Samuel, you can't treat me like this. How could you lock up all the food in the house? You don't want me to eat?" As soon as those words left my mouth, I instantly regretted saying it.

I saw the rage flash across his face as he crossed the room and grabbed me by my neck. "You have one more time to talk to me like you're crazy little girl. If you want to stay in this house, you're going to have to work." He said as he spit in my face and strike me down. The next thing I could recall was that the room went black.

When I became conscious of what had happened, I realized that I was in my bedroom. As the feeling started coming back to my body, I noticed that I couldn't move my hands and my feet. As I turned my head to try to figure out what was going on, I realized that my hands and feet were shackled to all four bed posts and I was completely naked. All I could do was scream.

I saw a slight movement to the left of my bed, so I turned to see what it was. Uncle Samuel was standing there naked looking down at me. He had that same far out look in his eyes that he always had when I caught him in my room. I tried calling to him, but I knew he wouldn't respond. It was like he was sleep walking.

"Uncle Samuel? Uncle Samuel? Are you alright? What are you doing? Why am I tied up?" I fired the questions back to back; I was really in panic mode. Instead of answering my questions, he slowly walked toward my bed as he played with his fully erect penis. "Uncle Samuel, please wake up!" I pleaded with him, "Don't do this Uncle Samuel. Please!"

He crawled onto the bed and continuously tried to ram his unprotected huge dick into me. After several attempts, he finally got his way with me. I screamed out in pain.

He was really taking my virginity. How could this be happening? How could I be getting raped by my uncle? Why was he doing this?

He started kissing me all over my body as he pounded away at my insides. Every time he would go for my lips, I would turn my head away from him. I couldn't believe that this was my first sexual experience. The more Uncle Samuel thrusted, the more tears fell from my eyes and rolled down my cheeks. Suddenly, everything went black again.

When I woke up, it was dark in my room. I looked at the clock and it read 9:09 pm. The events that took place earlier began to creep its way back to the forefront of my mind. I sat straight up and realized that the restraints where gone. As I sat up, I looked down and saw that my sheets were stained with dried up blood. I quickly rushed to the bathroom and began throwing up.

I was so disgusted, and I still couldn't believe that Uncle Samuel had raped me. I turned the shower on and just stood in the hot water hoping it would wash away everything that happened to me. No matter how many times I scrubbed my body, I still felt so dirty. After about thirty minutes in the shower I finally noticed that the water was burning my skin. I stepped out the shower and placed an Aloe Vera gel all over my body to take away the burning. I made sure I covered my body from head to toe just in case Uncle Samuel decided to come back for round two. My train of thought was all obscured.

I grabbed my flashlight and went through the linen closet in search of some thick curtains and new bed sheets. I came across two dark black light blocking curtains and some tacks. I went back to my room, grabbed a chair, and hung both curtains up over my door-less frame. As I took off the blood-stained sheets and placed the new sheets on the bed, it was at that moment that I decided I wouldn't stay here that long as I had initially bargained.

On Sunday morning, I woke up and walked down to the nearest store. I grabbed the Sunday paper and walked down to the park. As I sat in the park, I turned to the classified ads. My goal was to find me a job so that I could make some money and run away. There was certainly no way was I going to continue to live with Uncle Samuel. There were a few job ads that I liked, but being that I was seventeen, there wasn't a whole lot that I could do without parental consent. The job description that stuck out to me the most was one of an older lady who was looking for someone to take care of her mother for four hours per day. It sounded like the perfect job for me.

A few hours later, I made the trek back to Uncle Samuels's house. As soon as I stepped into the house, I felt a tirade of punches hitting my body. "Where the fuck were you, Amber? Did I tell you to leave this house?" Uncle Samuel screamed as he continued throwing punches all over my thin framed body.

Instinct kicked in and I began shielding my body from the blows. He finally got tired and stopped hitting me.

"Uncle Samuel, I walked down to the store to get a paper. Then I went to the park to look at the job ads. I will turn eightenn in two weeks and I would like to start working." I said weakly. Uncle Samuel stormed off without another word. What was with this man? He really is crazy. I thought to myself.

I composed myself then went to the phone in the living room to call and apply for the job. Mrs. Perkins sounded like a sweet lady. She told me to stop by tomorrow after school and we would do the interview. If she liked me, she said that I could start on Tuesday. I took down her address and hung up the phone. I later realized that she lived five houses down from Uncle Samuel's house. I couldn't wait until tomorrow; it was full of possibilities. I laid down and took a nap, making sure that the curtain was pulled closed.

I quickly awoke from my nap when I felt that eerie feeling come over me. As I opened my eyes, I saw Uncle Samuel standing not far from my bed talking with this stranger. The stranger was about 5'5, looked to be about thirty years old, had an olive complexion, and had this grotesque blond beard growing from his chin.

He had on a pair of tan slacks, a dark blue button-down collared shirt, and an off-white tie around his neck. I tried to sit up, but quickly realized that once again I was constrained to the bed. I was so caught up in watching them that I didn't even realize my dress was partially up, exposing a part of my panties.

My mind automatically went into panic mode. "Uncle Samuel, please don't do this. Mr. please don't be a part of this. Help me! I don't want this!"

Both men looked at me as if I was speaking a foreign language. Uncle Samuel slowly walked over, grabbed my face, and forced a handkerchief down my throat.

He walked back over to the man and said, "How much are you willing to pay for her?"

The man gave me another once over and mumbled, "I'll give you $200 for her Samuel".

Money? No, Uncle Samuel was not selling me to this man! He can't possibly be that crazy.

Uncle Samuel was quiet for a few minutes as he pondered what the man said. "Give me $250 for her Ted and you can fuck her for as long as you want this time. I popped her cherry yesterday, so you don't have to worry about that. She's clean and she's only been with me. If you give me $300 you can do whatever you like to her, as long as you don't bruise her up or kill her."

I turned back toward the man, hoping that he would come to his senses and call the police.

Instead of being concerned, this evil grin came across his face, "Sold. I'll give you $300 to make her my little slut." He pulled out his wallet and sifted through his money. Out came three crispy $100 bills that he handed to Uncle Samuel. Uncle Samuel examined the money, found it up to his expectations, and then walked out.

Before he got to the door he yelled, "Have fun Ted. Amber don't you do anything to ruin this or I'll kill you."

I immediately tried to let out a scream, but it was muffled due to the handkerchief in my mouth. I began crying and shaking my head as Joe began undressing. Deep down inside I knew he could see the terror written all over my face.

"Hey beautiful." He said as he slowly undressed. I turned my head away and looked at the clock. It was 6:00 pm. I cringed as his hand caressed my leg. I continued shaking my head signaling a 'no' to let him know that this wasn't what I wanted.

Ted continued to ignore my unwillingness to go through with this plan that him and Uncle Samuel had orchestrated. He slowly began kissing me all over my left thigh. I squeezed my thighs together as tight as I could. Why did I have to wear a dress today?

Next thing I know, I felt his wet tongue licking his way up my thighs. When he got to the place where my dress started to open, he paused and licked his lips. "This is what I want right here, I hope you're ready for this."

As soon as he said that, I knew he was going to go through with this.

Aggressively, he pulled my legs wide open and held them in place with his arms. Instead of pulling my panties down, he blew his hot breath on them. What the hell was he doing I thought to myself. A few more minutes of doing that, and my body started feeling weird. Was my body betraying me and getting turned on?

As my panty became moist, he whispered, "I knew you would like that." He pulled my panties to the side and inhaled my essence. "You smell good Amber; I bet you taste just as good too. Give daddy a little taste." He said huskily. He stuck one of his fingers inside me. "Damn, Samuel was right, you do have that bomb pussy. It's so tight." He said satisfactorily. I closed my eyes and waited for this horror story to be over.

Suddenly, I felt his tongue probing in my most restricted area. This was a new feeling for me; no one had ever done this before. I tried to keep reminding my mind and body that this was wrong, and that I didn't want it. The more I tried to battle them, the more my body started having these sensations. Ted was down there working magic with his tongue and it felt so damn good. He could tell that my body liked what he was doing with the way it began to shake. What was happening to me? My body started convulsing and then it became extremely relaxed. Did I just experience an orgasm? I thought to myself.

Ted came up from between my legs and licked his lips as he said, "Damn girl, you came all over my face." He slowly crawled up on top of me and inserted his dick inside of me. My breath caught in my throat. It felt so good when he slid it in.

Keeping up his slow pace, he constantly thrust his dick in and out of me. He could tell that I was enjoying it. He reached up and took the handkerchief out of my mouth as he said, "Don't you dare scream, Amber. Just take this big daddy dick. You know you're enjoying it." I was so thankful that he had taken that handkerchief out of my mouth that I let out a deep sigh of relief.

"There you go!" he said as he thrust once more into me, mistaking my sigh as a sign of enjoyment.

Ted switched up the tempo on me and sped up. Before I could stop myself, moans were escaping my lips, betraying me. I didn't want this;

he was taking advantage of me, but why was my body enjoying this? Next thing I know, my body began convulsing again. What the hell I said to myself as I laid there exhausted.

He pulled out and said, "I'm about to cum!" He brought his dick above my face and began jacking off onto it. I jumped when his bodily fluids landed on my hair, eyes, nose, and mouth. This was so disrespectful. I thought. All I could think about was him leaving. Please, hurry up and leave.

Ted must have heard my silent plea because he immediately got up and got dressed. He headed toward the door, then turned back around and undid my restraints. He smiled at me and said, "Until the next time Amber. I can tell you enjoyed that as much as I did."

As soon as he walked out the room, I rushed to the bathroom. As I began filling the bathtub with hot water, the bathroom filled up with steam. I just sat on the toilet sobbing and thinking about what just happened to me.

Why was this happening to me? How could Uncle Samuel allow someone to pay him to have sex with his seventeen-year-old niece? He was a very sadistic man.

How could my body enjoy that? Ted made me have an orgasm twice. Didn't my body know that it was just raped? Why did he make me feel so good?

I hated myself for how I felt. I slowly climbed into the tub and let my tears mingle with the water, Ted's semen, and the filth that I felt. After about twenty minutes, I climbed out of the tub and went to bed.

School was very uneventful that Monday morning. As soon as the bell rung to release us for the day, I ran to the bus stop because of the interview I was going to have that day. When I got home, I changed out of my school clothes and put on a pretty dress to wear to my interview. After I was satisfied with my interview attire, I started walking down the street to Mrs. Perkins house.

It was a beautiful two-story red brick house. They had about two acres of land filled with beautiful flowers. I walked up the four steps and rang the doorbell. One minute later, an older white woman answered the door. She was about 5'4, grey hair, soft blue eyes that had a hint of laughter in them and seemed to be about forty years old. She wore a soft blue and white collared dress and had on some black loafers. When she saw me, she face displayed the biggest smile. "Hello darling, you must be Amber. I'm

Mrs. Perkins, please come in." she said in the sweetest voice. She stepped back and let me enter the house.

Inside was a huge stark white foyer filled with old black and white photographs. Mrs. Perkins closed the door and then led the way to the kitchen. When we entered the kitchen, I immediately fell in love. This was my dream kitchen. The counters were a deep brown and black marble; she had an island in the center of the kitchen with red pots and pans hanging from them island, and the stools for her bar where black with square seats and silver legs. On the counter, she had small glass angels strategically placed, which intermixed with the beautiful lilies. "Mrs. Perkins, your home is beautiful." I exclaimed.

"Thank you, Amber. Please have a seat on one of the stools." She said as she grabbed two cups and poured us some tea. Then, she pulled out two saucers from the cabinet and placed a slice of apple pie and two scoops of vanilla ice cream on each saucer.

As she handed me a saucer, I said, "Thank you so much. This pie smells delicious."

Mrs. Perkins sat down two stools away from me and watched me for a moment.

After she took a bite of her pie and ice cream, she said, "Tell me a little about yourself, Amber."

I knew this was coming. What was I supposed to say? My dad killed himself and my mom. I moved here to live with my uncle who rapes and sells me for sex? No, that wouldn't work, she won't hire me then.

I smiled and said, "I'm Amber McGee, I will turn eighteen years old next week, and I recently moved here. I live with my Uncle Samuel down the street; he's the gynecologist down at the Women's Clinic on 13th Street.

My father killed my mother, and then shortly after, he took his own life. Uncle Samuel is my only living relative, so I had no choice but to come live with him since I'm a minor. I am in the 12th grade and I have no problems with my current school. My goals in life are to attend college, become a hair stylist, and one day open my own hair salon. My current hobbies are reading, writing, and drawing. I'm interested in this job because I enjoy helping other people. Mama always taught me that older people should be treated with kindness and that I should soak up as much wisdom from them as I can. I've never taken care of an elderly person for hours at a time, but Mama and I did use to go down to the Senior Residence and sit with them for hours."

Mrs. Perkins sat back and looked at me in amazement, "You have a good head on your shoulders, Amber. I would love you to help with my mother. Her name is Mrs. Sandy. You can start tomorrow, sweetheart. I wish you the best with your dreams and goals. It's unfortunate about your parents also, and I'm sorry about your loss.

Dr. Stewart is a good man and will take good care of you. If you ever need anything, please don't hesitate to come over and ask. I'm a great listener and I've been told that I give pretty sound advice as well." As I finished eating my pie and ice-cream, Mrs. Perkins told me more about her and her mother. I left the interview feeling like I've known her and her mother all of my life.

I took the two-minute walk home and reveled at my first successful interview. I was so caught up in my thoughts that I almost didn't notice the blue Porsche parked in the driveway. It wasn't until I had bumped into it, that I noticed it. My heart immediately started thumping.

I hope this wasn't one of Uncle Samuel's friends coming to have sex with me. I looked at the windows of the house to make sure no one was looking for me and I quickly walked by the house. I decided to go sit in the park for a few hours to give the person time to leave. As I sat there, I thought about Uncle Samuel and the unknown visitor. I really do hope that wasn't a person that had come to have sex with me. If it was, then Uncle Samuel was going to be furious that I didn't show up. I pray that he doesn't end up putting his hands on me when I got home.

Three hours later, I slowly walked back to the house and saw that the blue Porsche was gone. I tried to enter the house quietly, but Uncle Samuel had pulled a chair into the foyer and was sitting there facing the door.

My first instinct was to turn and run, but I didn't have anywhere to go. "Hello, Uncle Samuel" I said trying to play it cool.

Instead of returning my greeting he stood up and said, "Where were you, Amber?"

I could feel the fear consume my body as I said, "Today is the day I had my interview for the job. Remember, I told you on Sunday that I had an interview today. You told me that I can't live here if I don't have a job. I got the job, Uncle Samuel! After I left the interview, I went to the park to enjoy this beautiful day."

I slowly walked toward him so I could go to my room. Unfortunately, as soon as I tried to walk past him, he grabbed my arm. "Uncle Samuel, will you please let go of my arm? I'm about to get my things ready for school tomorrow." I pleaded.

30

Without letting go of my arm he said, "Take off all of your clothes."

My head whipped around as I said, "Uncle Samuel? Please, don't do this!"

He repeated himself in that same eerie voice, I knew something bad was about to happen.

"Uncle Samuel, please! Just let me go to my room." I pleaded.

He gripped my arm even tighter as he said, "Take off your fucking clothes, Amber! Don't make me say it again or it will be ten times worse."

Instantly, I started sobbing as I slowly took my clothes off, pleading with him not to do whatever he was about to do. I stood there naked, trying to cover myself and he started barking commands at me.

"Walk back down the foyer, turn around, and come back and stand a foot in front of me." He said.

"Uncle Samuel," I tried pleading one more time.

He let go of my arm and backhanded me across my face. "Shut up, you little slut and do what I say." He said forcefully.

I walked down the foyer as he instructed, turned back, and stood one foot from him. I watched in horror as he eyed every inch of my body.

"Bring your ass over here." He said.

I slowly walked toward him. He reached his hands up and caressed my breasts. He pulled me closer and started sucking on my nipples. My body automatically stiffened. As he sucked on my breast, he inserted his finger into my delicate spot. Unlike my body's reaction when Ted touched me, my body had the complete opposite effect.

After he finished violating me, he made me turn around and bend over. I heard him stand up and scoot the chair back. Then, I felt the most excruciating pain on my ass. I let out a loud heart retching scream as I turned and looked at him.

He had a long thick wand in his hand with red tassels hanging from it. He swung at my ass again and I screamed. "Uncle Samuel, stop! Please stop! This is not right! That hurts! Why are you doing this?" Instead of answering me, he hit me again. I fell on the floor writhing in agony. I heard him grab the chair and walk away.

Slowly I pulled myself up off the ground, grabbed my clothes, and slowly walked to my room. My ass stung so bad, that I couldn't even sit down. I fell onto my bed and cried myself to sleep.

One week later, my 18th birthday rolled around and I wasn't even joyous. It was just another day without my mama. Another day in which Uncle Samuel would make money by having Ted come over to fuck me. From the first time I'd seen Ted to my eighteenth birthday, I'd seen Ted a total of ten times.

Ten times, he fucked me in every imaginable position. Ten times I started off hating it, and ten times my body ended up enjoying it. Ten times Ted paid Uncle Samuel $300 to have his way with me. When would this nightmare end?

I wore the cutest outfit I had in my closet for my eighteenth birthday, which was this beautiful mint and pink colored knee length floral dress. I paired it with a pair of Cerise pink heels that brought out the pink in my dress and took the time to straighten my hair. I received so many compliments on my appearance that day. Overall, the day wasn't that bad because the few friends I had made sure it was a special day for me.

When I got home, I was surprised to see the blue Porsche there again. Uncle Samuels's car was not there, so I wasn't sure why the Porsche was there. Since it was my birthday Mrs. Perkins had given me the day off. I slowly walked into the house and went into my room.

When I walked into my room, I saw Ted laying on my bed butt ass naked. "Hey baby girl, he said. happy birthday!"

I quickly started shaking my head to signal a 'no.' "Not on my birthday. How could Uncle Samuel do this to me?" I mumbled.

He chuckled and said, "I have a birthday gift for you Amber. I'm pretty sure you will enjoy it. Get naked. Samuel told me that there will be repercussions if you don't oblige me. He doesn't seem to be in a good mood today either."

I slowly got undressed and walked over to where Ted patted my bed at. He told me to lie down on my stomach. He reached on to my bedside table and grabbed some massage oil. I was so frazzled by seeing him in my room that I didn't even notice the items he had on my nightstand. He poured the cold oil on my back and began massaging it into my skin. The more he massaged, the more the oil heated up. I won't lie; he was making my back feel damn good. This was my first massage ever.

I told myself that I might as well enjoy this since there was nothing I could do about it. As he massaged my back, I began to relax and enjoy the sensation. Within a few minutes, I had dosed off; I didn't even realize it until I heard him calling my name and telling me to turn over. I did as he said and laid there while he massaged the front of my body. After he finished, he took a bottle from the nightstand and started opening it.

"What's that?" I asked curiously.

He laughed at my innocence and said, "It's a flavored clit stimulator". He rubbed it on my clit and began blowing on it. It automatically began heating up. I had a feeling that he was about to turn me out.

He slowly began licking on my clit ever so gently. The more he licked, the more my body started tingling. That flavored clit stimulator was really doing the trick. Within minutes my body was rocked by a major orgasm. He licked my juices from his lips and slowly started kissing my body until he got to my nipples.

He slowly licked, teased, and pinched at my nipples until they were rock hard. Then he reached under my pillow and pulled out a medium sized funny shaped black thing. I had no clue what it was, and I was surprised that I didn't feel it while it was still under my pillow.

"Uhm, wha...what is that?" I stuttered.

A creepy smile came across his face as he whispered, "It's an anal plug. I've always wanted to try one of these out on a woman. Turn around Amber." I tried to protest but he placed his finger on my lips and said, "Don't even waste your breath. We're trying this. Turn over now! I'm going to lube it and place it in. Try to relax your muscles as much as you can."

Reluctantly I did as he said. I felt him start teasing my anus with a wet moist finger. He slowly inserted it in and out a few times as if he was teasing me.

Suddenly, I felt the rubber slowly inserted into my ass. It was the most uncomfortable thing that I'd ever felt. My body was screaming at me that this didn't belong at all. Nothing was supposed to be inserted in my ass, since it was for disposing of waste only.

Once I started to relax my body, the pain subsided. I felt Ted fumbling with the plug once he had inserted it in completely. I wondered what he was doing back there. Next thing I know, the plug started vibrating. I was not expecting that. Ted told me to turn around and lay down on my back. After I did what he said, he climbed on top of me and inserted his manhood into me. One thing I can say about having sex with Ted is that his manhood fit me perfectly. It's like my cave was made for his boat to dock in.

Ted slowly began pumping in and out of me. By this time, I was soaking wet. The anal plug was driving me wild. He placed his lips on mine and I could taste my juices. It made me remember how his juices tasted on my lips. Stop it Amber, I thought to myself.

He took both of my legs and placed them over his shoulders. The depth of his strokes and the vibrations from the anal plug had my body crashing as I rode each wave of my orgasm. I laid there exhausted, hoping that the session was over. Boy, was I wrong! He had the stamina of an athlete today. He had already busted one nut, but he still wanted some more.

He had me flip over and get on all fours. He turned the anal plug off and slowly removed it from my ass. He replaced the plug with his dick. I was surprised it slide in so easily; I guess that plug really loosened my hole up.

He started off slowly pumping in and out of my ass. This doesn't feel that bad I thought to myself. Ted reached up with both of his hands and placed them around my neck. Please, don't let him kill me I thought.

He used my neck like it was a harness and he started ramming his dick in and out of me like he was angry. I tried matching his rhythm and throwing my ass back, but he yelled at me to be still and take that dick. So, I kept my body still and let him have his way with me. Five minutes later, he busted his load all over my ass.

He slowly crawled off me and began getting dressed. After he was dressed, he looked at me and said, "Get dressed and come down to my car. I have a surprise for your, Amber."

I quickly cleaned myself up and went downstairs to meet him at his car. When I walked outside, he was standing by his open truck. I anxiously walked over to his trunk hoping he wasn't about to put me in it.

When I looked down in the trunk my mouth gaped open. Inside of the trunk was nine huge shopping bags from various stores and one large unmarked brown bag. The only bag I recognized was the pink and white bag from Victoria's Secret.

When I looked up at Ted, he was looking back at me smiling. I smiled at him and said, "Thank you Ted. This is so sweet of you."

He quickly responded, "You're welcome, Amber. You deserve more than this. I'm sorry your Uncle Samuel is putting you through this. Let's take these bags in the house."

Ted helped me carry the bags up to my room, he kissed me on the lips passionately, and then left me to discover my gifts.

Excitedly I began opening the bags. The first two bags were from Michael Kors; inside the first bag was a lovely black and red leather purse. Inside the second bag was an even more beautiful white and black leather purse. The next two gift bags were from Oscar de la Renta; inside the first bag was the most beautiful silk floor length beige dress I had ever seen in my life. It was absolutely gorgeous. Inside the second Oscar de la Renta bag was an even more gorgeous black knee length lace dress adorned with silver jewels around the deep v neckline. The following three bags were packed full of trendy clothes from Nordstrom. Upon opening the two Victoria Secrets bags I was surprised to see the variety of lingerie that he had brought. Never in my wildest dream did I imagine owning lingerie at eighteen.

When I got to the unmarked brown paper bag, I was curious to see what was inside. As I picked it up off the bed, it felt extremely heavy. Trying to contain my curiosity, I opened the bag and almost passed out.

Inside were stacks of 100-dollar bills banded together. I quickly counted how many stacks were in the bag and came up with a grand total of 100 stacks. I wasn't a drug dealer, so I had to get on Google and see how much money was in one band of $100 bills. My eyes bulged out of my socket when Google revealed that one band of $100 bills were equivalent to $10,000. A quick mental calculation of the total amount of money in that brown bag made me pass out almost immediately.

Next thing I know, I was waking up from the floor dazed. I had really passed out from being overly excited. My mind could not fathom the fact that I had $1,000,000 in my possession. I remember that there was a card at the bottom of the bag. I slowly pulled myself up and opened the card. It read:

To my dearest Amber,

I'm sorry that your life has turned out this way. Life is full of obstacles and you never know what cards you will be dealt with. I am so sorry that I participated in the wrong doing that your Uncle Samuel placed you in. My consciousness finally won, and I have decided to help you escape. I've been stuck in a loveless and sexless marriage for years, it finally started to take a toll on me. When your Uncle Samuel approached me with the proposition, I couldn't pass it up. Once I met you, I could tell that you were just an innocent little girl. You are so beautiful and seems like you have a good head on your shoulders. I can tell you don't like living there at your Uncle Samuel's house. So, I wanted to help you out. Here is $1,000,000 to help you get far away from him. As much as I don't want to see you go, I don't want to see you unhappy either. I wish you the best of luck in your endeavors Amber.

Love,
Ted

P.S.
If you ever need anything please don't hesitate to call me. 228-757-8493

I sat on my floor and cried. In an odd way, this was the sweetest thing anyone had ever done for me. After 10 minutes of sitting there bawling my eyes out, I began packing my bags. I decided to take two large suitcases, and a duffle bag. That way it would just look like I'm going on vacation, and transportation officials won't give me any problems since I had just turned eighteen.

As I walked into my closest, I struggled deciding on what to pack. From the last few months of daydreaming about running away, I decided to move to Macon, Georgia. With the money that Ted gave me, I would finally be able to open the beauty salon that I wanted with no worries of how I was going to sustain financially.

I pushed the suitcases in the back of my closest and decided to get online. I went to the greyhound website and looked to see when the last bus would be leaving from Biloxi. I figured I would go two cities over to catch the bus, just in case Uncle Samuel came looking for me. The last bus was leaving at 12:00 am. I purchased my tickets online and went in Uncle Samuels's office to print them out. Next, I called and reserved a cab for 10:45 pm. It would take roughly thirty-three minutes to get to Biloxi, so leaving a little earlier would give me time just in case there were any hitches in my plan.

After I finished packing, I showered and got into bed. I was so excited that the only way I could conceal it was to sleep. I turned my phone on to vibrate and set my alarm for 10:15pm. I was finally leaving this horrid place. Making plans for my new live was exhausting, so I closed my eyes and fell asleep.

Suddenly, I was woken up out of my sleep by an angry Uncle Samuel. "Wake up you ugly little bitch!" he screamed violently at me. Once I shook the sleep off me, I noticed the smell of alcohol wafting from his body.

"Did Ted come over and treat you like the good little slut that you are? Did he shower you with his cum? Answer me bitch!" I knew this was about to be something that I did not want to be a part of. I weighed my options in my mind and decided to play it cool. He was drunk and I did not want him to beat on me tonight.

Slowly I responded, "Yes, Uncle Samuel, Ted came over and treated me like a good little slut. I did everything he wanted me to."

This nasty grin spread across Uncle Samuel's face as he began undressing in my doorway. No! I thought to myself, not again. He slowly walked toward me than sat at the foot of my bed.

"Come over here and suck my dick bitch." he said in this creepy voice.

As soon as I opened my mouth to protest, he slapped me across the face with all his force. He hit me so hard that I went falling over sideways, right onto the floor. Tears automatically started rolling down my cheeks as I began to cry.

"Uncle Samuel, please don't do this. I'm your niece. It's not supposed to be this way." I pleaded as I continued to cry.

He quickly jumped off the bed and grabbed me by my hair. Through gritted teeth, he said, "If you don't suck my dick right now, I will kill you."

Something deep down in my soul knew he wasn't playing when he said that. He pulled me by my hair and pushed my mouth down on his exposed dick. With tears streaming down my face, I started sucking Uncle Samuels's dick. He kept his hand intertwined within my hair so he could direct my every move. A few minutes later, groans became flowing from his mouth.

"Yes Laura, yes! You remember just the way I like it. I missed your mouth on my dick. You've always been the best dick sucker that I've ever had." he said in that creepy voice that he used earlier.

I stopped sucking his dick once it registered in my mind what he had just said. I know he wasn't talking about my mother. He forced my head back down on his dick.

"You've always been my favorite fuck. Why did you leave me, Laura? Our love was pure and genuine. It didn't matter what everyone said about us. I love you! I wanted to help you take care of the baby. Why won't you let me be a father to her? I told you before that John isn't good enough to be a father to her. Amber is my daughter and you need to let me help you take care of her. Let's be the family that we deserve to be."

I threw up all on his dick. I could not believe the words that I had just heard leave his mouth. He's my father? There was no way my mother was his sister if they were fucking. He slapped me as hard as he could.

"What the fuck is wrong with you bitch! You just threw up on my fucking dick. Come clean this shit up!" he yelled angrily. I quickly backed away from him.

"Uncle Samuel, are you my father?" I screamed at him as I continued backing away from him.

He looked at me confused, "Of course, I'm not your father Laura. I'm Amber's father." My heart fell out of my chest as I blacked out in front of the only exit in the room.

I awoke to my alarm going off, reminding me that it was time to get ready to leave this place for good. I still can't believe Uncle Samuel was my father. Everyone would always talk about how much I resembled my mother, but I could never see it. It was bad enough he was forcing me to perform sexual acts with him while he was my uncle, but it's even worse now that I found out he was my father. What the hell was my mother thinking? Did they both have mental issues to engage themselves in incest? I wonder if Uncle Samuel raped my mother like he did to me. I shuddered at the thought.

As I walked into my closet to get my suitcases, I listened carefully to ensure that Uncle Samuel was not still up. I didn't hear any noises at all coming from within the house. So, I picked up both suitcases, and my duffle bag and peered out of my room. Looking around, I didn't see light emitting from the living room neither did I see light shining under Uncle Samuel's door. Ever so slowly I tiptoed out my room and down the stairs, stopping every few steps, listening and waiting. Once I made it to the front door, I looked back one more time taking in the scenery. Hopefully, this was the last time I had to see this horrid place. I opened the door as quietly as I could and shut the door on my past.

Deception

4 CARLOS

Stepping outside I felt a wave of relieve take over my being. The frigid air brushed against my face as if it was embracing my escape. I quickly carried the suitcases down the driveway and started walking down the street toward the convenience store.

Once I was a good distance away, I placed the suitcases down and pulled them toward my destination. Just as I got to the closed convenience store, the taxi was pulling up. I quickly walked up to the cab and told him that I was the one that called. The short Latina taxi driver stepped out of the car and helped me put my bags into the trunk. As I climbed into the back of the taxi and settled in, I couldn't believe that I was this committed to running away. Fuck it, I had to get out of here.

Luckily, the bus terminal wasn't busy at all. At this point, the vendors there were shutting down and going home for the night. This was the last bus leaving the station for the night, so the workers were rushing everyone to get on the bus. They were so anxious to get home that no one asked to see my identification, and I was able to just get on the bus with no problems. The whole time I was waiting for the bus to leave the station I was hoping and praying that Uncle Samuel didn't show up and drag me off this bus. I kept looking around nervously trying not to be suspicious. Finally, after fifteen grueling minutes, the bus pulled out from the station.

I kept my eyes trained out of the window hoping that I didn't see one of Uncle Samuel's cars racing beside the bus. When it looked like the cost was clear, I wrapped my purse around my body and stuck it behind my back just in case someone decided that they wanted to try to steal from me.

Watching the shadows dance around the bus I finally drifted off to sleep.

I awoke to someone shaking me. Quickly, I jumped up trying to shake off the grogginess. The bus driver was standing in front of me. Once he was certain that I was coherent, he told me that I had thirty minutes to get something to eat and be back on the bus before he departed. Slowly, I gathered my belongings and climbed from the bus; it was still dark. I looked down at my watch and was shocked to see that it was 3:45 am. I must have been tired. Looking around my surroundings, I saw that there was a McDonalds inside of the terminal. I decided that I would use the restroom, stretch my legs, then get McDonalds to go.

After I got back on the bus, I thanked the bus driver and found my way back to my seat. There were a lot more people on the bus now than there was before. As I sat down, I decided to check my itinerary. We were currently in Montgomery, Alabama, which means that there was only 2.5 more hours left on my trip.

As I sat eating my Sausage McGriddle, my mind replayed the events that took place over the past few months. I still couldn't believe that so much had transpired. Praise the Lord that I was finally free from Uncle Samuel and his psychotic ways. It's still hard for me to grasp the concept that he is my real father. I always had a feeling about John, but my mother swore up and down that John was my biological father. Besides, he never treated me like he didn't love me. I wonder if Uncle Samuel used to rape my mother like he did me. I hope that's the case because I can't possibly believe that my mother would willingly sleep with her brother. If so, my family is truly messed up. I wondered if that was the reason that I never met any of my other family members over the years. My brain was having a troublesome time grasping the whole mother and Uncle Samuel fiasco, so I turned my thoughts toward Macon, Georgia until I drifted off to sleep again.

My eyes slowly fluttered open as I felt the bus breaking and heard the bus driver's voice come over the speaker. I finally made it to Macon, Georgia. Excitedly, I gathered my things and I was ready for this new adventure. When I got off the bus I looked around at my new dark surroundings. Wow, I was really in Georgia. Reality started to creep in as I walked toward the inside of the bus terminal. I had no game plan.

I knew that I wanted to buy a shop and start a hair salon, but where was I going to live? Anxiety started to rear its ugly head. I quickly walked into the terminal looking for a phone book. After finding the motel section, I found a Motel 6. Luckily, they had an opening when I called, so I made a reservation. I didn't have a credit card, so I couldn't get an Uber. I thumbed through the phone book again until I found and ordered a taxi.

Fifteen minutes later, the taxi arrived, and I was on my way to the motel. Ten minutes later, I saw the motel 6 sign looming in the air. If I would have known it was this close, I would have walked. Pulling up to the motel, I became worried that I wouldn't be able to get the room since I had just turned eighteen. I wasn't sure if the legal age was eighteen or twenty-one to rent a room. I told the taxi driver to wait outside for me while I ran inside.

When I got to the front desk, I was greeted by a big busty red head. She gave me the biggest smile as she asked how she could help me. Nervously, I walked up to the counter and told her that I had a reservation for an Amber. She gave me a once-over and asked to see some identification. I reluctantly pulled out my drivers permit and handed it to her.

After reviewing my license, she handed it back and said that I barely made the cutoff to reserve a room. She then proceeded to tell me that she would need a major credit card to put on file. Tears welled up in my eyes and she automatically looked uncomfortable. As the tears slid down my face, I leaned onto the counter and told her that my uncle was raping me and I had to run away. I didn't have a major credit card on file and that I just needed a place to stay for five nights. I could see the horror spread across her face as she started shaking her head to indicate that the answer was no.

As she stood there watching the tears fall from my eyes, she said she could reserve a room for me for only two nights since on the third night she wouldn't be working. Her only stipulations were that I had to pay her in cash and that I couldn't let the other workers now that I was there. I quickly agreed and thanked her for her kindness. She gave me a room in the back of the hotel and told me to just leave the key in the room when I checked out. I walked outside wiping the tears from my eyes.

The taxi driver jumped out the car and pulled my suitcases out the trunk. I paid the fare and left him a generous tip. Dragging my suitcases, I walked around the outside of the building until I came to my room. Walking into the room, I was highly disappointed, but extremely grateful at the same time. I placed my bags in the corner and searched for the delivery menu. After ordering my food, I climbed into the shower and washed away the funk from my road trip. I must have stayed in the shower longer than normal because just as I was getting dressing, there was a knock on the room door. I opened the door, paid for my food, then sat down on the bed to enjoy my pancakes and eggs. I didn't realize how hungry I was, but I swear I devoured that food within five minutes.

After I ate, I grabbed my laptop and jumped online. My goal was to find an apartment as quickly as possible. After hours of searching, I had narrowed it down between Windy Hill Manor Apartments and Terrace Apartments. For the price, these were the best options and they came fully furnished. Today would be a busy day for me, I thought to myself. Apartment hunting, car shopping, and cell phone shopping. Becoming an established adult is arduous work and very expensive. This money won't last forever, I need to find me a job.

Five hours later, I awoke to the maid cart rolling by outside. Slowly I crawled out the bed, ordered some breakfast, and called a cab after I finished eating. The first place that I went to was Jimellis Audi Marietta. Last night, I had found this bad 2015 Audi for $28,000 that I needed in my life.

When I walked in, a short cocoa colored African American man walked up to me. He introduced himself and gave me his car salesman spill. I listened politely until he finished, and I told him exactly what car I was here for. His eyes narrowed as he asked me where my parents where. Looking at him dead in his eyes, I responded, "My parents are away on a business trip currently.

Skeptically he replied, "Ma'am, you will have to have your parents here to cosign."

I started laughing and replied, "Don't worry, I don't need a cosigner. I'm going to pay cash for it. I did a lot of research, so my parents gave me the money that I needed."

His eyes began to budge out of his head. "Well, let me show you to the car" he replied slowly. He took my driver's permit and returned with the key.

Walking up to the car, I knew it was the one I wanted. It was a 2015 glacier white Audi A3 1.8T Premium plus Sedan with chestnut brown leather seats. There was 6,838 miles on it and had only one previous owner. It was fully loaded with navigation, Audi connect, parking system, rearview camera, moonroof, and had a LED interior lighting package. As I took it on a test drive, I decided that I wasn't leaving this lot without this car.

After the test drive, Mike, the sale's associate, asked me what I thought. I could not contain my excitement as I squealed, "I'll take it". That concerned look came over his face as he replied, "Are you sure you don't need a cosigner for this car?"

I smiled as I responded, "Don't worry about it Mike. Trust me, my family is well off and I am going to pay cash for the car."

As we walked back inside, he invited me to his desk and told me to have a seat. After we filled out the paperwork, he gave me the grand total and stared at me waiting to see my reaction. I pulled out my wallet and counted $31,000. I laughed to myself as his mouth dropped at the sight of all that cash. I handed him the money and watched as he sat there and counted it. After he made sure that everything was in order, he had me sign the papers then handed me the keys to my new Audi.

As I was walking out the door, Mike cleared his throat and said, "Ms. McGee, this is unprofessional, but do you mind if I call you sometimes?" As I turned around to look at him, he nervously adjusted his light blue tie.

I flashed him the most flirtatious smile that I could muster and said, "That is very unprofessional of you Mike. How do you think your boss will feel about you coming on to an eighteen-year-old?" He began stuttering out a response, but I cut him off. "You can't call me Mike, but I can take your number and call you".

A smile crept across his face as he wrote his cellphone number down on the back of his business card. "I'm glad you changed your mind, otherwise I would have to take the car back since you only have a learners permit." He said slyly.

I glared at him wondering if he was serious or not.

"Damn woman, you had me sweating. I hope to hear from you soon." He muttered.

I flashed him another smile, took his business card, and walked out the door to my new ride.

As I sat behind the wheel, I was overwhelmed with joy. This was truly a blessing from God. No way in hell would I have ever thought that I would flat out own a 2015 Audi. Ted had really hooked me up when he gave me all this cash.

After I plugged the address in for the first apartment, I adjusted the radio station and drove off. When I looked back at the dealership, I could see Mike standing at the door watching me drive off. I laughed as I remembered the look on his face when I pulled out the cash. He was kind of cute, and I might give him a call sometime soon.

Fifteen minutes later, I pulled up to Terrace apartment complex. Just looking at the area, I was a little skeptical. There were bars over some of the apartment windows and broken-down cars in the parking lot. As I drove through the complex some more, I noticed that there were some men standing behind a building looking like they were up to no good. I quickly plugged in the address to the next apartment complex. There was no way in hell I was living in a place like that. I can't believe this shit, that website did the apartment so much justice.

Driving to the next apartment, I noticed that the apartment was in a much nicer neighborhood. When I pulled up, I was immediately placed at ease. Hopefully, this apartment will meet my expectations, I thought to myself.

Instead of getting out and going inside, I drove to the nearest Walmart and sat in the parking lot. Being that I was eighteen with no job, no major credit card, nor a debit card, I knew that I needed someone to sign the lease for me. I sat in the parking lot for an hour trying to find the perfect candidate to help me with my scheming. Just as I was about to call it quits, I noticed this nerdy looking black guy walking toward the store. This was my one and only chance to get this right. I got out the car and slowly followed behind him inside.

He was around 5'5 with some khaki cargo pants on and a maroon logo less shirt. He had the look of a man longing for a lovely lady to make his day.

I waited until he turned down the body wash aisle and was staring intently at the choices laid out before him. Slowly, I walked up to where he was standing, grabbed some Axe body wash and said, "I think this will smell nice on you."

He looked around confused. "Are you talking to me?"

I looked down the aisle like he had done, then replied, "Of course. There isn't anyone else on this aisle."

He let out a nervous chuckle then said, "Well, I guess I'll take your word on it. My name is Carlos by the way."

He reached out his hand to grab the body wash from me as I introduced myself. I couldn't help to notice how adorable he was up close and personal.

His complexion was as smooth as a glazed Krispy Kreme donut. There was no acne or blemishes on his face at all. He had dark riveting brown eyes that drew me in. His nose was perfectly formed like a dollop of daisy from the sour cream commercial. Those beautiful pink lips drew me in begging for me to kiss them. I caught myself staring at him, so I had to snap out of it quickly. Get yourself together Amber, this is pure business.

"I'm new to town and I'm trying to find a place to live. You wouldn't happen to have any suggestions, would you?" I asked him as I took a step away from him.

He gave me a confused half smile and started naming off some places that he had heard good things about. It was just my luck that one of the places that he named off was the apartment that I wanted to go see.

"It's funny that you said Windy Hill Manor Apartments. I was thinking about visiting there after I leave here."

An impish look filled his eyes as he said, "Well, if you need some company, I wouldn't mind escorting you there. A beautiful woman like yourself shouldn't be out here alone. Are you alone?"

Something about the way he asked was I alone sent chills up and down my spine. I really needed to use him though, so I brushed that feeling to the side.

"I am alone. I wouldn't want you to cancel your plans to help me view an apartment though."

He quickly responded," It's no bother at all. Luckily for you, I didn't have any plans today."

I smiled flirtatiously and said, "You're such a gentleman."

He chuckled as he said, "I get that often. How about we finish shopping and meet at the front door in 15 minutes."

I agreed and went on my way. I picked up a few necessities and checked out. As I walked to the door, I saw him standing there with four bags in hand.

When he saw me walking toward him, he smiled. I could see the nervousness written all over his face.

As I got closer, he said, "I didn't think you would show up."

I smiled and walked right past him.

"Amber!" he said.

I laughed and responded, "I'm just playing. I'm parked on aisle seven. I'm in the white Audi. How about you meet me there and I'll follow you."

That impish look returned to his eyes, "An Audi huh? I can see you're a classy woman. I drive a red beamer. Let's do this."

We went our separate ways when we got to the parking lot. As I walked to my car, I kept asking myself if I was making the right decision. I convinced myself that I was and got into my car.

When we arrived at Windy Hill Manor Apartments, nervousness consumed my body. What in the hell was going on with me? As we walked inside and was greeted by the staff, I did all the talking. After introductions and a brief spill of what I was looking for, Heather, the attendant, grabbed two sets of keys and led the way.

The first apartment she showed us was a fully furnished studio apartment that was nice as hell. I instantly fell in love with it. The walls were painted a light tan color with a nice deep red accent wall. The couches were black with accented red pillows adorning them. The wooden floors were heated and had a huge tan and red area rug underneath the couches. Walking into the kitchen there were brown and black marble counters with plenty of counter space and a huge dining room area. As I walked toward the bedroom area, I noticed a queen size black canopy bed atop a black and red area rug.

In the bedroom nook, there were two matching black dressers and a full-length body mirror along the wall. Walking into the bathroom I immediately noticed the glass enclosed walk in shower beside the brick enclosed bathtub. My mind was made up, I wanted this studio apartment. I told her that I wanted to convene with my boyfriend and that we would come back inside once we decide. She asked if we wanted to see the second apartment, but I refused. As she walked us to the door, she told us that she would be in her office and to just let her know what we decide on.

Once we made it back to the parking lot, Carlos turned to me and said confused, "Boyfriend? Why did you introduce me as your boyfriend?"

Slowly, I lowered my head in embarrassment as I said, "I have to be honest with your Carlos. I'm eighteen and I need someone who has credit established, a debit and/or a credit card, and work history. If you do this for me, I will give you $250 after the lease is signed."

Quickly, I raised my eyes to him to watch his reaction. I saw even more confusion cross his face as he slowly backed away from me. "Sign a lease for you! Where the hell are your parents?"

Sadly, I responded, "They are both dead. My father killed my mother, then turned around and killed himself on the same night. It's not something that I want to relive right now. Please, I need your help. I don't have anyone else." As soon as those words left my mouth, I instantly regretted them.

The look that came across Carlo's face was terrifying. I guess he noticed my reaction and quickly fixed his face. I could see him thinking as he pulled out a Black & Mild cigar out of his pocket and lit it up.

He puffed on it then offered it to me. I adamantly refused his offer. After he inhaled and blew out the smoke, he turned to me and spoke softly, "I'll make a deal with you. I'll let you keep your $250 if you let me move in with you. I've been trying to save up some money to get my own place, but the initial deposit along with the background check and first months' rent is too much for me right now."

I started shaking my head no, indicating that I wasn't interested in his offer. "I'm sorry Carlos, I'm not ready for roommates right now. I just want my own place, besides, it's a one-bedroom apartment with only one bed in there. Where would you sleep?"

An eerie look came over his face as he said, "With you! Just playing. I'd sleep on the pull-out sofa in the living room area. It would only be for six months while I build my funds. I'm a pretty clean guy and I will give you your privacy when you request it."

The thought circulated around my mind. As I stood there weighing the pro's and the con's they balanced each other out. This was a complete stranger that was requesting that he moved in with me. I mean, I guess it was no different than him just cosigning the lease. He could take me to court and the law would be on his side since his name was on the lease. No Amber, I thought to myself. You don't know this guy from jack shit, he could possibly be crazy. There's something about him that was off.

"No, I'm sorry. I don't know you like that to be living with you. Won't you reconsider and just take the $250? What if I upped it to $350?" I asked pleadingly. He turned away from me and started walking to his car. "Where are you going?" I yelled out after him.

Without turning around, he responded, "No lease if you don't allow me to be your roommate."

Tears welled up in my eyes as I realized that my only hope was agreeing with his absurd request. I quickly starting walking to his car that was getting ready to pull off. Calm down Amber, I told myself. How bad would it be to share your place with him for six months? You could get a few of those room dividers and separate the bedroom. He couldn't possibly be that bad. Just say yes so you can have a place to live.

Carlos!" I yelled out. "Okay, but only on a few conditions. I mean it Carlos! You'll have to agree or the deals off the table."

He rolled down his cars window and turned toward me, "And what are those?" He said with a satisfactory smirk on his face.

Shit, I said to myself. What were my conditions? As I walked toward him, I gathered my thoughts, "One: you cannot enter my bedroom portion without permission from me. Two: no smoking in the house. Three: you cannot have anyone over without discussing it with me first. Four: you must help keep the house clean and we each are responsible for buying our own food. Five: we will not steal from each other or eat something that doesn't belong to us. Six: you must pay your half of the rent on time."

He stood there thinking for a few seconds then he said, "I'm the one co-signing the lease, I will have to be the one to lay down the terms. Luckily for you, those are very reasonable. It's a deal."

I patted myself on the back for successfully negotiating with him, however, I couldn't shake the feeling that I was making a deal with the devil. Something about him was off. I told him to give me a few minutes while I go to my car to count the money that we would need. The last thing I needed was for him to rob me blind. I gave Carlos the money for the security deposit, first month's rent, and the application fee. He was genuinely surprised when I handed him the stack of money.

All he could say was, "Damn girl. Where did you get this kind of money from? You rich or something?"

I ignored him and told him to go take care of business. I let him take lead on the conversation with Heather and signed when it was time for me to. After Carlos and I signed a 1-year lease, we exchanged numbers. I would be responsible for picking the keys up to our new apartment tomorrow. It was decided that he would move his stuff in two months from now. This would allow me to get my things situated. What had I really done by agreeing to be roommates with him?

The next day, I gathered all of my belongings, placed them back into the suitcase, and headed to pick up the keys to my new residence. It was the same lady as yesterday, and so she greeted me and handed me the keys along with a bottle of cheap champagne. I thanked her then went to my new home. As I walked in, I dropped my suitcases by the door and walked around while admiring my new residence. I'm finally living life like an adult. Now all that was left for me to do was to find a job.

I had put a decent dent in all the money that Ted had given to me. I sat down on the bed and calculated the cost of my rent for the entire year. Carlos would only be here for an interval of six months, so I needed to make sure that I was able keep a roof over my head. Looking around every corner of the apartment, I needed to find a place to stash my money. A few places came to my mind, but I felt like they would be too obvious if someone was looking for my money.

After searching through the living room, dining room, and my bedroom, there were only two options left for me to choose from: the bathroom or the kitchen. I figured that I could put the money into the vent in the bathroom like I one time saw on a movie; but if I saw that movie, I'm sure someone else saw it too. So, I opted for the kitchen, but where in the kitchen?

I opened the cabinets and checked the floorboards, but nothing was acceptable to me. Finally, my eyes settled on the washer and dryer. How can you use the washer and dryer to your benefit Amber? Think girl think.

Slowly, I walked over to the laundry room area and started examining it. The laundry room is a perfect place because washing clothes is a valid excuse to go in there. I pulled out both the washer and dryer away from the wall as I examined the exposed area. I decided to split the money up and place them in flat bags and tape them directly to the back of the washer and dryer. Carlos had no business moving the washer and dryer away from that position. This would have to do for the mean time until I'm able to find an alternative location.

I spent the next two months in search of jobs and checking out vacant buildings for my hair salon. Carlos still hadn't moved into our apartment yet. He was well overdue to grace our new home with his presence. I wondered if he was alright, but a part of me hoped that he never showed up.

As I lay out on my bed making a list of some vacant buildings, I heard the front door jingle. Automatically, I jumped up and quickly walked to the kitchen to grab a knife. Just then the doorbell rang, and I heard Carlos call my name. Relieved, yet disappointed as I went to open the door.

"I'm glad I caught you while you were here shorty." He said as he barged into our new apartment.

Damn man, I thought to myself, I wish he didn't show up. I was really hoping that he had totally changed his mind about moving in with me.

Interrupting my thoughts, he said, "Where do I put my stuff roomie?" Begrudgingly I pointed over toward the living room area. I went and sat on the bed and watched as he hauled his stuff in. Luckily, all he had were clothes, shoes, a 32-inch TV, and a PlayStation 3. This was perfect to an extent, now I wouldn't have to worry much about him turning this place into a pigsty.

Carlos finished bringing all his belongings in the house within three trips. As good as I thought that was, I still couldn't help but think what a damn shame it was that a grown man of his standard didn't have that many belongings. Lord, please don't let this man be childish.

After Carlos finished putting his things away, he opened a bottle of

Hennessey and poured me a cup. I had never drunk alcohol before in my life, so I didn't know what to expect after it all. As I tasted the dark brown liquor I immediately chocked and spit it out.

"This shit is nasty as hell!" I exclaimed loudly as I placed the cup on the counter. As I looked at Carlos, I instantly regretted my actions. A vision of Uncle Samuel beating my ass flashed across my eyes when I noticed the same evil look on Carlos's face.

"I'm sorry!" quickly came out of my mouth as I tried to rectify the situation before it got any worse. "This is my first-time consuming alcohol and my didn't know how to react. I promise it won't happen again."

As he glared at me, I could see the gears in his mind turning. The look disappeared from his face as he watched me intently. "It's alright this time. Don't you ever do no fuck shit like that again Amber! You do not waste a black man's Henny."

I wiped the sweat form my brow as I let out a breath of fresh air. I was saved by grace, because initially Carlos looked like he was about to murder my ass. From that moment forth, I vowed to myself that I would be more conscious and careful of the things that I said and did around him. Carlos could possibly carry the same crazy genes that Uncle Samuel have. The darkness that flashed across their faces screamed domestic violence. I don't want to ever get on his bad side.

I spent the next two weeks actively searching for a building to buy so I could open my hair salon. Most days, I would leave the house at 9:00 am and wouldn't return until 3:00 pm. Everyday Carlos would watch me leave the house, and he was always there when I returned. Always in the same spot; sitting in front of the TV playing video games. Every night his cellphone went off around 9:00 pm. He would put on a pair of starched down blue jeans, a t-shirt, his gold chain, a pair of Jordan's, and a hat that complimented his shoes. What the hell could he be doing during that time dressed like that? I know that he didn't have a real job, but somehow, he managed to always give me his half of the rent on time. I stayed up until 3:00 am one night trying to see what time he would return home. By 3:05 am he still wasn't home, so I fell asleep.

For ten months things were very uneventful in my life. No one would take my offer on the buildings in my location that I found suitable to establish Hairlicious Designz. My nineteenth birthday was in two months and I still wasn't any step closer in making my dreams a reality. Carlos hadn't moved out in the six months like he promised, so I was stuck listening to his excuses as to why. For the past nine months, I'd been stuck working this low-end job at Hungry Earls as a cashier. I don't know how people can work at a fast food restaurant day after day. Within five days of working there, I was already sick of it. It just wasn't for me. I'm going to own my own business and be successful. My phone ringing brought me out of my depressing thoughts.

I didn't recognize the 478-area code that was calling, so I put on my professional voice as I answered the phone. After listening to the person on the line talk, I could barely contain my excitement. One of the properties that I had looked at in the past had accepted my offer. I would go to the bank tomorrow to sign the papers and pick up the property keys to what would be my new salon. I wasn't a religious person, but whoever was up there surely did answer my prayer that I had put out into the universe. My life was finally starting to fall in line with my dreams. I laid out my clothes for the next day and went to bed.

5 NO FUCKS GIVEN

It seems like a few minutes after I dozed off, I was awakened by the sound of glass shattering and what I could have sworn was a woman giggling. I immediately shook the grogginess off and hopped up and went into the living room. I quickly darted to the light switch and turned it on.

As my eyes scanned through the room, they landed on a naked Carlos in the kitchen and this beautiful naked dark African goddess lying carelessly on the couch. She quickly covered up her genitals as an embarrassed smile washed across her face. We both turned and looked at Carlos. I was waiting for an explanation and the African goddess awaiting him to put an end to her embarrassment.

We were both taken aback when he gently walked straight to the couch with all his glory hanging out, sat down, and asked me did I want to join in. I was so shocked that I just stood there with my mouth hanging wide open. Before I could even gain my composure, the beautiful naked dark African goddess began gathering her belongings as she began speaking in Spanish.

I watched as her naked breasts bounced around her chest with every move that she made. Slowly, my eyes began etching her image into my brain. Her curly brownish red hair that fell in a mass of curls framing her face. Those almond shaped eyes that looked like they came off a damn baby doll. Her medium sized kissable lips that looked as inviting as an open house. The way her body curved ever so gently in all the right spots had me wanting to reach my hands in between her perfectly shaved legs and attempt to play a melody with not only my fingers, but with my tongue as well.

"Excuse me," I heard her mutter in broken English. "You block door" she stated.

Quickly I regained my composure. "I'm sorry.... what's your name?" I asked genuinely.

Confusion swept across her face as she looked from me to Carlos then back to me again. "Na-tal-e-a" she enunciated in that sexy accent.

"Natalea" I repeated, "Nice to meet you Natalea. I'm Amber." I said with a heartwarming smile. She reached out to shake my hand and I was amazed at how soft and smooth her hand was when it glued to mine. She was the true definition of an exotic woman.

"I sorry for wake up, it was accident. Do you mind if I take your cellular number to call you so I can replace your glass?" she asked wholeheartedly.

I wonder where she was from. I could tell from some of her broken sentences that she was still trying to master the English language. My motives were not really pure, but I agreed to give my number to her. After I gave her my information she turned and walked out of the door.

Now that she was gone, I felt like I could breathe again. As I turned to head back to my bed, I remembered that Carlos was still sitting there completely naked. He must have been watching me because when I looked at him our eyes met.

Instead of apologizing he said, "Why don't you come over here and finish what she started since you ran her off?" I scoffed at him in disgust.

"There has never been any sexual chemistry between us, and I hope that I haven't given off that vibe." I said with my best black girl attitude.

He chuckled and continued drinking his Hennessey.

As I laid in bed, my mind drifted back to that gorgeous black woman. From her accent, I think it is safe to assume that she was from Dominican Republic. I could not get her etched image out of my mind, coupled with those dark chocolate titties bouncing up and down around her chest as she tried to gather her composure. I could just imagine myself running my hands through her soft curly hair; I bet it smelt like fresh coconut and flowers. I had the visions of my face buried between her legs, and my hair gathered in between her fingers as she yelled out in pure ecstasy. I glanced over at Carlos to see if he was looking my way. Luckily, he was engrossed in the television watching ESPN.

Slowly, I slide my right hand down my body until it rested on top of my baby blue silken panties from Victoria's Secret. I could feel the heat illuminating out from my yoni as my juices began to saturate the thin layer of the material. No Amber, I told myself. Don't do it, Carlos is right over there. What if he hears you or turns around and catches you? Can you imagine how mortified you'll be?

As I laid there trying to reason with myself, my yoni pulsated beckoning me to come play with it. The calling was so strong that I threw all cautions to the wind. Once again, I glanced over at Carlos to see if he was watching me. He wasn't so I cautiously slide my panties to the side. No longer able to control myself, I slowly ran my fingers up and down my vulva collecting the sweet nectar as if I was a hard-working bee. I quickly brought my finger to my mouth and sucked the juices off like a hungry newborn.

Anxiously, I returned to the task at hand then I slipped another finger inside of me as I closed my eyes and imagined that the African Goddess was the one playing with my yoni. Slowly, I moved my other hand onto my right breast and began caressing my nipple. Alternating between breasts, I licked my fingers and moistened my nipples as I continued rubbing them softly.

Bringing my breast up to my bended head I slowly flicked my tongue over my already sensitive nipples. A few minutes later, I stopped thrusting my fingers in and out of my yoni, and afterwards I turned my concentration on my clit. I used the juice from my yoni to rub it across my clit. Slowly, I rubbed back and forth until I couldn't take it anymore. I quickly began rubbing my clit faster until I felt the waves wash over me. At the height of the wave I let out a satisfactory moan that seemed to travel up from my soul. Realizing how loud that moan was, I laid eerily still trying to pretend that I was fast asleep. I heard the TV pause and I heard Carlos softly call my name.

There was no way in hell I was about to acknowledge him. He called my name a few more times until he gave up and continued watching TV again. I let out a quiet sigh of relief as I closed my eyes and proceeded to fall asleep.

A few hours later, my body began waking up as it became turned on again. The feeling of hands caressing and teasing my breast continued as I slowly woke up from my sleep. Reluctantly, I opened my eyes and I began to scream.

"Shut the fuck up bitch!" I heard as a hand tightly covered my mouth to smuggle my screams. Without thinking any further, I bit down on the hand that was covering my mouth. He let out a guttural growl as he brought forth his other hand down to slap me across the face.

"Don't you ever do no shit like that again bitch. I will end your life! Open those pretty little legs up for daddy".

When I didn't comply with his request, he slapped me even harder than before. "I'm not playing with you, you dirty little whore, open your motherfucking legs! Don't make me tell you again Amber!"

Slowly, I opened my legs as I had a flash back of Uncle Samuel putting his hands on me.

As my attacker slide his bare penis inside of my precious yoni, I began to cry. I could not believe that he was doing this to me. What did I ever do to him to deserve this?

I was brought back to the present when he muttered, "I heard you over here getting yourself off earlier. That was an indication to me that you wanted some real dick in your life, not no damn fingers." My rapist said to me drunkenly.

"Carlos please sto-," before I could finish my sentence his hand came across my face again. This blow harder than the last.

"Shut the fuck up bitch and take this dick!" he said angrily.

Tears began flowing down my cheeks. I never trusted Carlos one bit, but I never thought that he would end up raping me either. I should have listened to my gut feelings the first time I got an uneasy feeling about him. As I lay there stiff as a board, I thought back to Uncle Samuel raping me and selling off my body to Ted. What the hell was wrong with men? Did I have a tattoo on my forehead that said rape me? Do I look that vulnerable that men feel like they can take advantage of me?

"Why me Lord, why?" I screamed in agony. I saw Carlo's head come down on mine as an agonizing pain swept through my head right before I blacked out.

As I came to, everything that had happened flashed before my eyes. Carlos brutally raping me because I had messed up his sex shindig earlier. Carlos slapping me countless times for protesting against him raping me, and finally him head butting me until I lost consciousness because I screamed out "Why me Lord?"

What kind of trifling shit was that? I always had a feeling that Carlos wasn't shit, but I never had any proof. The day I poured out my cup of Hennessey without drinking it should have been an indicator of what was to come.

Damn Amber, I thought to myself, not again. My eyes quickly darted across the room to ensure that Carlos wasn't coming back for more of what he stole. I noticed his legs dangling over the side of the couch and him snoring softly. Climbing out of the bed and being careful not to make a noise, I tiptoed into the kitchen.

As quietly as I could, I opened the kitchen drawer which contained a variety of knives in it. Examining all the knives, I selected the sharpest one in the drawer. Pausing, I stood still staring at the stainless-steel knife and trying to ensure that he wasn't going to wake up. After he didn't move for a few minutes, I crept over to where he was sleeping and stood over him deeply lost in thought. The still voice in my head reared its head.

"Amber," it said to me, "don't do this girl. If you do this, you will go to jail for a very long time." Then the evil twin voice piped up with a voice louder than ever before. "Amber, think about everything that has happened to you. Do you really think this will be the only time he rapes you if you continue living here? Kill this motherfucker and let's leave the state. No one will ever know. Your name is on the lease, but you no one can discredit the fact that you moved out on your own months ago. Just kill the motherfucker. Fuck that nigga."

Without hesitation, I sliced Carlos's throat in one swift movement, then I proceeded to plunge the knife deep into his chest cavity. His eyes quickly shot opened as blood began gushing out from his throat. Slowly, I pulled the knife out as I watched the life drain from his eyes. Unbeknownst to me, images of everything that Uncle Samuel had done to me began playing like a movie behind my eyelids.

Without thinking any further, I repeatedly stabbed Carlos until I fell on the floor winded. I sat there for what seemed like hours trying to figure out what I had just done and how I was going to get away with it. Finally, a great calm came over me as I realized what had to be done. I stood up and went straight to the kitchen to wet a towel with soap and water. I began wiping the murder weapon down and erasing all traces of my fingerprints. From underneath the sink, I grabbed the bleach and poured it into the sink. Placing the knife into the sink full of bleach, I watched as it soaked.

Breaking my trance, I went to the bathroom and took a shower getting rid of all the traces of his blood. After I showered, I placed the bloody clothes inside of a trash bag and placed it by the door. Next, I began throwing all of my belongings that I had in my suitcases and a few trash bags.

I peeked outside of the door to make sure that no one was around the neighborhood. The coast was clear, so I began filing up my Audi with everything that I had to my name. Once I was finished, I took some Clorox Wipes and wiped down everything in the house that I had ever touched; including the shower and I even pulled my hair out of the drain. After I had all the trash in one bag, the knife in another bag, and my money that I had hidden a while ago in another, I closed the door with my hand covered in gloves and walked away from my old life. Once I got to the car, I decided to run back inside and take whatever money that he had on him.

When I searched his pants for his wallet, I was amazed at how bulged out it was. As soon as I pulled it out, I saw that it was full of money. Without counting it I took the whole wallet and dashed out of the house. I made sure to leave the door unlocked so the door wouldn't be locked from the outside. Fuck Carlos, I said to myself as I pulled out of the parking lot. That nigga wasn't shit and he wasn't ever going to be shit.

I drove until I came upon a park on the other side of town. I pulled into the parking lot and turned my headlights off. It wasn't until I had taken a deep breath that I realized that tears were falling from my eyes. I sat there crying until all that sadness had left my body. This faggot raped me and here I am sitting and crying my eyes out for him. Fuck that nigga. I need to put myself back together.

It was like a switch went off in my head. I stopped thinking about Carlos and started concentrating on what the hell I was about to do next. Did I want to stay here and go sign the papers to own my very own business tomorrow or did I want to leave the state and start anew? If I left the state it would be harder for the cops to find me if I ever became a suspect. Suspect! What am I thinking, Carlos didn't have a real job, and no one would come looking for him for days. Hell, no one would probably come looking for anyone until the rent was due, or his body started smelling. That African Goddess was the first person that he had ever brought over to the house. Regardless of the fact, how am I going to find a place to live?

The location for the salon was two cities over so possibly I could live there. Naw, I told myself, fuck that shit. Let's go to Savannah.

I googled hotels in Savannah, Ga, and plugged the first address I came upon into the navigation system. As I pulled out of the parking lot and headed to the interstate, I reminded myself that there wasn't anything here for me. Fuck Macon I thought to myself.

LIFE ANEW

6 A FRESH START

Two hours and twenty-two minutes later, I reached Savannah City Limits. I stopped at the first motel that I came to and attempted to get a room there. The name of this hotel was You + Two. Which automatically led me to believe this was a sleazy hotel. Being that I was still eighteen with no major credit card, I knew for sure that I would have to flirt my way into a room.

As soon as I walked into the lobby the stench of cigarettes, beer, and latex wafted into my nose. My immediate thought was to leave this place at once. It's only going to be for a few days Amber, it's going to be hard to find someplace else. It's only temporary, I thought to myself again.

Scanning through my surroundings, I noticed a tall, skinny, ginger headed white man behind the counter to my left. Slowly, I walked over to the counter and stood there patiently. He was so engrossed in his magazine that he didn't even notice my presence. As I looked closely to see what held his interest so heavily, I saw that it was a porn magazine. Two beautiful melanin sisters stood there naked and posing seductively. I cleared my throat loudly.

Startled, he threw the magazine to the side and stood up and tried to hide my view of it. "Welcome to You +Two where anyone can freely do the do. How may I help you ma'am?" He said in a nasally voice.

"Hi, I'm trying to get a room for the night" I said sweetly.

He cocked his head to the side as he eyed me up and down, "I'll need to see some identification miss".

Reluctantly, I reached in my wallet and retrieved my driver's license. As he took it from my hand, I watched his every move. After examining the license, he handed it back to me and stated, "You have to be 21 or older to rent a room here. I'm sorry ma'am."

Quickly I rambled off my depressing situation to him, but he was holding firm to his resolve that I was underage. As I turned and started walking away defeated, the image of that magazine that he was looking at flashed before my eyes. Putting on the most seductive smile that I could muster at that time I returned to the counter. Leaning on the counter so that he could see a hint of my 34 C titties, I leaned in and whispered to him, "How about I make you a deal big daddy." As the words big daddy left my lips, he turned as red as a strawberry. Yes! I thought to myself. I'm going to get this fucking room.

"What's the deal?" he stuttered.

Sensually, I licked my lips as I said, "You let me buy a room for tonight and I'll suck your dick right here, right now." I was amazed to see him turn an even darker shade of red. He glanced around as he thought about what I said to him.

"It's a deal. Come around the counter and sit underneath it." He said quickly.

I walked halfway around the counter then stopped and said, "Get me my room first". We stared at each other as we both tried to gain the upper hand in the situation. Finally, he looked away and started booking the room for me.

I placed my driver's license on the counter right in front of him and climbed underneath it. As I started fumbling around with his pants, I felt so disgusted. What the hell was I thinking? Was I really about to suck some random guys dick just to get a roof over my head tonight? Hell, I might as well because there's no way in hell that I would get a good night sleep by sleeping inside my car.

I've always been freaked out by the thought of fucking a random man. Ok Amber, it's not going to harm you. Just think of sucking his pink dick as a necessity for your comfort. It's a necessity for you to have a place to sleep. A necessity for you because you need a place to shower. It's only temporary. Hell, you might even enjoy it. Possibly get some potential side dick even though he is ugly as hell. I thought to myself. Let me just go ahead and get this over with.

He saw me fumbling with his pants so he slid them down and sat down on the chair so that no one coming toward the window could see what was going on underneath the counter. The rancid smell that attacked my nostrils was deafening. His dick smelt like musty forgotten basketball shorts in a gym bag. I sat back as I contemplated.

As I looked at this pink musty dick that stood erect in front of my face, I couldn't help but be disappointed at what I saw. Of all the dicks that I have had in my short sexual experience so far, this is by far was the smallest and smelliest one that I had ever seen. His dick was about the size of a little jug of jungle juice. It took everything in me not to ask him where the rest of it was.

Hell, this should be easy. He looked down angrily at me as he saw the hesitation boldly written on my face. Right before I put his little dick in my mouth, I told him to hand me my license and room key. He quickly obliged as he pushed my head onto his dick. I couldn't believe this shit; his dick didn't even fill up my mouth. This would be quick and an easy head. I slapped his hand away from my head and started sucking his Jungle Juice dick. Slowly, I licked the head of his dick, starting what I mostly like to call the moisturizer phase. Along the sides of his penis my tongue explored, moisturizing his dick so that my mouth would smoothly glide up and down his peg leg dick.

Once I was satisfied with how moist I had made his dick I went into the real work for the day. Slowly, I cupped my lips and slide his head in my mouth. A moan escaped his lips. Continuously, I put his dick in my mouth and pulled it out, suctioning more of it every time I put it in my mouth; I became a human vacuum. I was starting to get into it just when he screamed, "I'm cumming!' and I felt his load shoot into my mouth

How disappointing, I thought to myself. Quickly, I got up, wiped my mouth with my hand, and walked out just as an older white man walked in through the front door. I practically ran to the car and grabbed my overnight bag. I found my room and immediately turned on the shower to wash away more of my sins. As the shower water heated up, I brushed my teeth and gargled with mouthwash. What the fuck was I doing? I climbed into the shower as my thoughts continued. How the hell did I end up sucking someone's dick for a hotel room? A hotel room that I paid for…wait! He didn't even ask me for any form of payment. Oh well, I'll take a free hotel room. Hell, that's the least he can do for making me suck that rancid jungle juice of a dick.

Pink penises are starting to lose that good impression with me. I need some good dick in my life. Who am I fooling? I need a big black cock in my life. One that will have me chocking as I try to maneuver it down my throat. A big black cock that will make me moan as it slides into my sacred cave. One that will have me speaking in tongues as it beats down my walls. Hell yeah, I need to go on a man hunt.

As the warm shower water continued hitting my tired body, my mind began shutting down. Quickly, I washed off and got myself out of the shower. I was so exhausted that I didn't even have the energy to rub lotion on my Nubian skin. As soon as my head hit the pillow I was out.

The next morning, I awoke very confused as to where I was at. As I gathered my thoughts together, everything came flooding to the front of my mind. I had killed Carlos and had fled out of town. Within ten minutes of being in a new city, I had already sucked a musty dick just to get the keys to this rinky dink motel. I'm not even 21 yet, and I've already murdered someone and sold myself out. Lord I pray that the police don't link me to the scene of the crime; I'm too young and beautiful to go to jail. I'm not trying to get raped up in there. This was not the kind of life that I was trying to have. Oh well, I thought to myself. I might as well move on with my life, what's done is done.

First thing on my to do list, I needed to find a place to live. I would be nineteen in two more months, so I would have to put on a sob story to convince someone to let me rent with them in a more respectable community. Hopefully, this time I wouldn't have to trick out my body, but I was prepared to do it if I had to. Shit, some women just don't know the level of power that their pussy has over men. Reluctantly, I logged on to my laptop and began the search for a new home. Three hours later, I had narrowed it down to two prospective locations. I showered, got dressed, and hopped in my car all within twenty minutes.

As I pulled up to the first apartment I quickly fell in love with the location. It was right dab in the heart of the city and as I drove in, I saw a few vacant business locations. Slowly, I climbed out of the car and entered the leasing office. The first thing I noticed was the music that was coming out from the speakers in the ceiling. It was playing one of my favorite songs Solange: Mad ft. Lil Wayne. I heard a soft feminine voice say to me, "Hello there, how may I help you?" As I turned to face the voice I was mesmerized.

There she stood about 5'6 with soft Hershey brown skin. Chestnut brown eyes that glistened as the rays from the sun danced around them playfully; teasingly pulling me in. Her natural hair adorned her head in a beautiful, fresh looking twist-out. When she smiled at me those pearly whites let me know that she took good care of herself. Her ears where adorned with gold dangling earrings that matched the gold sun medallion that rested on her exposed cleavage. She had a beautiful lilac floral print sundress on, with white sandals that brought out the white designs in her dress.

"How may I help you?" she repeated.

"Hello" I said giving her the flirtiest smile I could muster at that moment. "I'm looking to see if ya'll have a one-bedroom apartment that is available?" I said kindly.

"You're in luck" she said, "We just had one open up two days ago."

I let out a sigh of relief, "Perfect! I would love to see it."

She walked straight to her desk as she said, "I would love to show you. Please come over here so I can get some information from you and then I will show you the studio. Do you have your ID on you?" I walked over to her desk and handed her my id. "I'm April by the way. And you're…" She looked down at my ID and said, "Amber. Nice to meet you Amber. I see that you are one year younger than me. Do you have someone that's going to cosign for you?"

O hell, here we go, I thought to myself. Here comes the time for me to put on like I'm going up for best actress award. I closed my eyes and mustered up some tears.

As the tears began to fall April gasped, "O no! What's wrong Amber?" The concern was so genuine in her voice that I knew my plan would work perfectly.

"I'm so sorry April. I told myself that I wouldn't cry anymore if I had to bring this up. I turn nineteen in two months and I'm an orphan. My mother and father passed away last year, which left me with my uncle. He raped me until I got fed up with it and ran away. Please overlook the fact that I don't have that much established credit. I swear to you I won't be an issue. I swear that I won't do anything to bring attention to myself."

The tears were gradually falling down her face as she said, "Oh you unfortunate thing! I am so sorry for your loss. Your uncle is a horrible person, did you call the cops on him?" She asked angrily.

I sucked in some snot as I said, "No. He's the only living relative that I have. If I would have called the cops, they would have sent me to an orphanage."

"You're absolutely right. How dumb of me. It's against our policy but we can work something out. Come with me so I can show you the one-bedroom apartment."

She got both of us some tissue and grabbed the keys to the

apartment. After we composed ourselves, we went to view the apartment. All I could say was that it was perfect. It was fully furnished, so I didn't have to worry myself about buying furniture or anything extra. The bedroom area was spacious and came with a king size bed. As I scoped out the closets, I was very impressed. "Spacious and walk-ins are two important aspects for me." I told her gently.

Light gray walls surrounded me which were adorned with red, black, and white décor. The black leather couches matched the color scheme perfectly. As I turned toward the bathroom area my mouth dropped. It had a nice walk in shower and a garden style tub beside it. In my head, I told myself that I was sold already, I didn't need to see anymore. I let April continue showing me the way as I watched her ass sway in that sundress. This is the perfect view, I thought to myself.

After we made it back to the office, I paid up the entire rent for a year. April stared at me dumbfounded as I counted the money. I told her that it was insurance money from my parent's deaths. Afterward, she gave me the key and I thanked her for her help. Before I could walk out of the door, she asked me if we could exchange contact information and told me that I could call her anytime. I gladly accepted. Calling her would be on my to do list once I got settled in. I did need to start making some friends out here.

I walked to my car and started bringing my things out and taking them inside of my new home. Excitement overcame me as I realized that this was going to be my first place all by myself. Ted doesn't know how big of a help he was by giving me all that money on my birthday last year. Without him, none of this would have been possible one bit. Hell, I probably would have still been getting raped by him and Uncle Samuel at will; being mistreated and abused. In two more months, I will be nineteen and I already have my own place. In a few weeks, I will open my own business and my dreams would finally come true.

As I made a few trips to bring my belongings in the house, I reflected on the past two years of my life. So much had happened. I was honestly surprised that I was still standing by myself. As I brought the last of my belongings into my new apartment, I thankfully looked around; I am so blessed I thought to myself. "Jesus please be a fence around me every day from here on out Lord" I said quietly to myself. Now to take care of business.

I grabbed my phone and called the number to the building that I wanted to check out for my business venture. By the time I got off the phone with the agency, our appointment was already set, and the realtor had told me all the details on the location. I would go in there tomorrow and walk out with the property all mine. Until then, I would take a nice refreshing bubble bath and get a good night's sleep.

The next day, I woke up refreshed and ready to conquer the world. The meeting with the realtor went well. Being that I was paying cash, there wasn't a lot of paperwork to do. I would have the keys to my new business the following week if there weren't any unforeseen delays. With that being taken care of, I could sit back, relax, and start dreaming about the name of my new Salon. I made a mental note to start ordering furniture and tools for my salon and to put out an ad for some workers to come in.

Logging on to the computer, I decided to put out the ad for beauticians first. I created a craigslist account and sat there staring at the screen. What in the world would this ad say? I sat staring at the screen for at least ten minutes before the right combination of words came into my head.

"Hairliscious Designz is a new salon that will open up in a few weeks in downtown Savannah. I am looking for talented/creative stylists to make Hairliscious Designz the safe haven for men and women alike as we pamper them and leave them feeling refreshed and brand new. If you are interested in creating this safe haven with me, respond to this post with your resume and a face shot".

As I posted the ad, I felt myself overwhelmed with excitement. There it was, another great step that I took to get my business off the ground. This was really happening. I copied the ad and posted it to a few different websites. Getting the word out there that I was looking for stylists for my salon was my utmost priority. After I get the stylists all squared away, I would focus on promoting my business. Mentally, I hyped myself up; continuing to encourage myself to press forward without being discouraged.

By the time I got off the computer, April was on my mind. What was it about this girl? I didn't think I was gay, but I really wanted to find out what her soft looking lips tasted like. Without putting much thought into it, I grabbed my cellphone and texted her.

Me: Hey April, how are you?

April: I'm doing great Amber, how are you?

Me: I'm making it. I'm a little lonely up here. Being new to an area can be tough when you don't know anyone.

April: Well lucky for you, you know me.

Me: Being that I just met you yesterday, I will admit that I want to get to know you.

April: O really?

Me: Yes really! Are you ok with that?

April: Of course. You seem like you're worth getting to know.

Me: Well thank you.

April: You're welcome beautiful. How about we start tonight?

Me: Meaning?

April: Dinner?

Me: Where at?

April: It's a surprise.

Me: I'm not a huge fan of surprises.

April: Trust me. The food will be delicious. Let's just say this is our first trust exercise.

Me: I don't like this, but ok.

April: Great! I'll pick you up at 8:00 pm. Wear something casual.

Me: Ok.

April: Ok. See you tonight.

  I laid there on my bed thinking about what had just transpired between us. Did she just ask me on a date, or did she ask me out as friends? I wonder if she likes to experiment with women? I have never willfully had sex with anyone before, would she be my first? All these feelings were so overwhelming. Times like this I wish I had a big sister to talk to. I glanced at the clock on the nightstand, it was 5:00 pm. I set my phone alarm for 7:00 pm and laid down and took a nap. Tonight, would be exciting, I thought to myself, hopefully I won't be too awkward.

  My alarm went off at 7:00 pm. Reluctantly, I got out of the bed and turned on the shower. As the water warmed up, I gathered my razor and shaving cream. I needed to properly shave the hair from my body just in case April and I ended up becoming intimate.

  Ten minutes later I stepped out of the shower feeling like a brand-new woman. Next, I sat on the bed and I applied Bath & Body Works cucumber melon lotion on my body. Walking to my closet I stared at the clothes I had taken from Uncle Samuel's house. I wish I could have taken all of the clothes that he had bought me, but I was only able to take two suitcases of my favorite outfits.

  April said dress casual so casual it was. I grabbed a pair of dark blue jeans and a light pink mid sleeve length shirt. I paired it with a silver cross necklace and a pair of silver hoop earrings. Looking at the clock, I realized that it was ten minutes till 8:00 pm. Quickly, I threw on some eyeliner, mascara, blush, and a nude lipstick. Luckily, my hair was already in a puff from earlier in the day, so I sprayed some water on it and pulled out some curls. After being satisfied with my appearance, I decided to put on some black pumps to complete the look. Just as I put on my last pump the doorbell rang.

 Slowly, I walked toward the door as if the man of my dreams was on the other side. As I opened the door, my heart began to flutter at the picture of beauty that stood before me.

 There she stood looking like an ebony Jet magazine beauty of the week. Her black and brown curls glistened as the light from my apartment hit it. April's makeup was bold and delicate. She had smoked her eyes out and had added a cat tail for a dramatic affect. Her lips were coated in burgundy paint and her cheeks showed a hint of color. The diamond earrings that she wore dangled down from her ears begging for attention. My eyes roamed down to her chest as I realized that she had on a black quarter sleeved dress that showed a decent amount of cleavage. Without thinking I licked my lips.

 She giggled as she said, "You like what you see?"

 I blushed as I said, "You look beautiful April." As I turned to walk away from the door to compose myself, I said, "I thought you said that we were to dress casual? Do I need to change?" As I turned to look back at her I saw her beautiful titties jiggle as she laughed.

 "This is my definition of casual Amber. You look beautiful, it's no need to change". I grabbed my purse and we walked out of the door.

 The next day I had a hangover from hell. My head was throbbing, and I could barely stand up to my feet without getting dizzy. All I could remember was that I had a blast with April last night. We had gone to this Thai restaurant on the outskirts of the city. It was my first-time eating Thai, but April promised that the food was good. She was absolutely right; the food was amazing. We decided to get a few different entrees and shared them, as we drank some wine.

 As I laid in the bed images of her replayed through my mind. She is so fucking beautiful. Her perfect white teeth with that enchanting smile had really done a number on me. Why was she having this effect on me? I rolled over to grab my phone and saw that I had an IMessage.

 "Good morning! How do you feel beautiful?" It read.

 I smiled as I texted her back. "Good morning Sunshine! I feel like shit today. I've never been so fucked up in my life."

Within a minute she had responded "I'm on the way to come take care of you."

I smiled as I texted her back "ok." I could not believe that she was going to come over and nurse me back to normal health. She is such a wonderful person.

Fifteen minutes later, I heard a knock on the door. Slowly, I made my way to the door to find a cheerful April on the other side. She hugged me tight as soon as she saw me. "I'm going to make you feel all better" she said in her cheery upbeat voice. April closed the door and walked straight into the kitchen. She placed the white plastic bag on the counter and began taking items out of it. Out of the bag came a jug of red Gatorade, wheat crackers, ginger root, honey, a lemon, and two big cans of chicken noodle soup. As I walked up to her, she handed me the Gatorade and told me to drink it. Something about her tone of voice told me that I better do what she said or there would be repercussions.

As she chopped the ginger, I slowly began drinking the Gatorade. My stomach felt so queasy that I had to quickly run to the toilet. Just as I let the toilet seat up, I began throwing up all my wrong doings from the night before. As my body began to sweat, I swore to myself that I would never drink so much ever again. After I finished throwing up, April brought me a cold towel and told me to lay down. Within in minutes sleep had consumed me.

My eyes fluttered open as I regained consciousness. What time is it, I thought to myself? As my eyes adjusted to the dimness in the room, I felt a body rustle to the right side of me. As I turned in bed, I saw April lying next to me in the bed and scrolling through her phone. When she felt me moving about, she turned and smiled at me. "How are you feeling princess?"

I laid my head back down as I pondered my response to the question. "You know, I feel a lot better. What time is it?"

April checked her phone as she said, "It's 7:15 pm." She laughed as a look of confusion came over my face. "Yes" she said, "You've been sleeping since 8:30 am." I began shaking my head in disbelief.

"Damn, I'm sorry beautiful." She wrapped her arms around me as she told me that it was not a problem. Gracefully, she climbed out of bed and heated up some soup for me. She watched me cautiously as I slowly ate my soup. After I finished, she took my bowl to the kitchen, rinsed it out, and proceeded toward the bathroom to run me some bath water. Without a word, my eyes followed her every move.

Once she had turned off my bath water, she beckoned me to her. I hugged her and thanked her for all her help. She reaffirmed to me that I didn't have to keep thanking her for anything. She reminded me that that's what friends are for. As she spoke to me, she grabbed my toothbrush, placed my charcoal whitening toothpaste on it, and handed it to me. I laughed as I began brushing my teeth. I had forgotten that I had thrown up all my life sins earlier. Afterwards, I undressed and climbed into the warm inviting bubble bath that she had ran for me.

She grabbed a chair and sat next to the bathtub. The way she was looking at me warmed my whole body and sent butterflies flying around in my stomach. "Amber," she said in a gentle voice "I enjoy your company." I smiled as I told her that I too enjoyed her company and that I appreciated everything that she had done for me so far. We sat there and talked for 20 minutes straight. It was so refreshing to have a girl friend to talk to in this way. I've always been alone; I didn't know that friendship could be so great.

April grabbed my loofah that was hanging on my faucet, poured some body wash onto it, and then dipped it into the water. I stared at her wondering if she was about to wash me off herself. My inner self wanted to protest, but my body just couldn't. Gently she took the loofah and started washing my back. I was so glad that she couldn't see the expression on my face. How tender she was being with me just melted my heart. Next, she washed my neck and both of my arms. As she ran the loofah over my breasts my nipples automatically stiffened like a guard in front of Buckingham Palace. Gently, she lifted each breast and washed under them both. I tried not to stare at her, but I couldn't help but appreciate this melanin queen.

As she washed my body, she never looked at my face. She intently focused on the task at hand. After she was done washing my legs, she finally turned and looked at me. "I'll leave the rest to you beautiful" she said to me. She proceeded to stand up and leave me in the privacy of my bathroom. Once I finished washing my yoni, I let the water out of the tub. How refreshing I thought to myself. As I looked around for my towel, I saw April walking in with it. She stopped directly in front of the tub and held it open for me. As I went to reach for it, she pulled it back from my reach and said, "let me do it." As I stepped out of the tub, she slowly began drying me off. If I didn't know any better, I would irrefutably say that she was checking me out.

As she wrapped the towel around my naked body, she grabbed my hand and led me to the bedroom. Once in there, she grabbed the lotion and started moisturizing my entire body. I sat there quietly watching her. Next, she removed the towel and continued applying lotions to those areas that were once hidden. I couldn't believe that I was sitting here naked and letting another woman outside of my mother baby me. What was I thinking? Once she finished, I stood up and gave her a big loving hug. As I dropped the embrace, I couldn't help myself as I leaned in and gently kissed her lips. What the hell was I thinking? I can't possibly like girls.

Instead of pulling away, April leaned in and deepened the kiss. Maybe I do like girls after all. As our lips separated, we both giggled. Instead of backing away from each other, she started kissing me on my neck. Once again, my nipples stood at attention. She pushed me down onto the bed as she said, "I see you like that." I just laughed nervously. There was a warmness that had crept over my body as it yearned to be touched. She climbed on top of me and started licking a trail down my body. A slow trail down my neckline until she came to the midpoint between my breasts. "Which one do you want me to tease first Amber? Left or right? Or would you prefer me to stop all together?"

Quickly, I opened my eyes as I yelled out, "No! Don't Stop." She laughed at my sudden outburst.

"Well which one do you want first beautiful?" She teasingly asked.

I couldn't decide so I just shrugged my shoulders. She hesitated then went toward the left side. Lightly, she brushed her tongue over my nipples. Slowly she began tracing circles around my areola and teasing my body as I silently begged for more. As she started sucking on my nipple a soft moan escaped my lips. This feels like heaven I thought to myself. This desire that I have inside…is this what consensual sex feels like? As she made her way to my other breast, she continuously teased my left breast with her fingers. This is amazing, I thought to myself.

After what seemed like eternity, she slowly kissed her way down to my wet waiting pussy. The anticipation that she had built up in my body was quite unbelievable. I just wanted to shove her head between my legs; but I refrained. Let her take her time I thought to myself. She planted tender kisses on the areas of my thigh closest to my yoni. Just get to it my mind screamed internally. Next, she placed kisses all over my pussy lips. When she parted my lips and stuck her tongue between them, another moan escaped my lips. Over and over, her tongue explored my most intimate parts, sending shivers up and down my spine. As she began sucking on my clit she reached up and started teasing my nipples once again. A current washed through my body as I screamed out in pleasure and my legs began to shake. Instead of letting me ride out the wave, she stuck her finger inside of me and began stroking my g-spot. I felt a warm liquid run down my ass as April began to laugh.

"O shit!" she said amused "I didn't know that you were a squirter." I chuckled nervously as I felt the puddle of liquid being deposited on the bed.

I looked at her embarrassed as I yelled "Oh my goodness. I did not mean to pee the bed."

April let out a loud laugh as she said, "You didn't pee the bed beautiful. When liquid leaves your body like that during sex it's called squirting. If you smell it, you'll see it's not urine. It's just an indication of how much you were enjoying yourself."

Nervously, I laughed as what she said processed in my mind. Thank God I didn't pee myself, I thought to myself. How embarrassing would that have been?

After she regained her composure she came up and kissed me passionately. It seemed like we made out for hours. Finally, she pulled away and said, "Now that I've had my appetizer, let's go get the main course."

Once she said that, I realized how hungry I was. "Yes" I said, "Now that I feel better let's due this." I got up and got dressed. Within fifteen minutes we were leaving the house. I was in paradise with April.

Over the next few days, I spent all my time preparing for the grand opening of Hairlicious Designz. Interviewing hairstylists, make up technicians, and barbers took a lot out of me. In the end, I ended up hiring four hairstylists, one makeup technician, and one barber. I decided that I would have a promotion for 50% off for the first twenty customers that patronized. Deep down in my heart I knew that this business would be successful. Finally, the grand opening was tomorrow morning.

The next day I woke up at 7:00 am sharp. I showered, brushed my teeth, and spent the next thirty minutes trying to figure out what I was going to wear. I settled for an all-white dress with some black stiletto heels. Hell, it was my grand opening, so I needed to make a very good first impression. As I packed my bag for the day, I made sure to put my flats in there. There was no way in hell that I was about to be doing hair in some stilettos for nine hours. I said a quick prayer as I walked out of the door.

When I eventually pulled up to the shop, I noticed the extensive queue that had formed outside of the building. It consisted of women, children, and men all hoping to be one of the ones to get the 50% off discount. As I walked to the building, I greeted everyone and told them that I was happy to see them and that the shop would open in 20 minutes. I had opted out of doing a ribbon cutting, I felt it was more appropriate to just flip the switch to the open sign. When I walked inside, my staff was standing by the window and was so excited about all the customers that we would have today. They cheered as I entered the building making me even more nervous than I was before. They were so anxious that they wanted to open the doors immediately. Instead, I opted for a pep talk reminding them of my expectations and how proud of them I was. I told my receptionist to take her place at the front of the counter as I walked to the doors. As my staff waited by their booths, I smiled at them, flipped the light sign on, and then opened the doors.

I greeted and shook every customer's hand that day. I was so thankful that my grand opening was a huge success. By the time the last customer left the salon, I was exhausted. I cleaned and closed the salon down and rushed home.

Overall, we had forty-five customers that day, but we were only able to service eighteen of them. A fair share of the customers being men due to haircuts taking lesser time to complete than weaves, braids and silk sets. For the women and children in line who did not get seen, I scheduled them appointments and promised to honor the 50% off coupon. This had us nearly fully booked for the rest of the week. Today was a good day, we made $500 total and that was including tips. I'd never been so proud of myself before. I wish I could call my mother and tell her about my day. Boy, do I miss her? After showering I crawled into bed and went straight to sleep.

In order to celebrate my first successful week, I decided to get out and have a little fun that weekend. I had seen an advertisement for the Reggae Festival and heard about it on the radio, it was supposed to be a dope event. April was working, so I decided to go and check it out by myself. The traffic getting there was hell, I took me twenty minutes to finally pull in and park. Climbing out of my SUV, I adjusted my long olive-green sundress, my thin golden belt around my waist, and checked my golden brown natural wavy hair in the reflection of my car. I have to admit that I was looking sexy as hell. Who knows, I might even find me a man out here.

As I waited in line to purchase a ticket, I decided to watch the various people that walked by. There were so many beautiful black women out there that I started fantasizing about starting a friendship with them just to be able to fuck them. Outside of April, I had no friends here, so sometimes I did get lonely. That was definitely something that I had to change; this was the perfect opportunity to try and meet some new people.

Finally, I reached the booth and purchased my ticket. Walking through the gate I was shocked to see so many booths and so many people out here. Slowly, I started walking down the first aisle while stopping to browse at the booths that caught my attention. Fifteen minutes in, I came across a table selling Bob Marley paraphernalia. No one knew this, but I was a huge fan of his. As I walked up to the table, I noticed a tall beautiful ebony sister standing there and looking at the merchandise on the table. When I stopped at the table our eyes met and I could tell straight from the bat that she was a kindred spirit.

She smiled at me with her perfectly straight pearly whites. As I started making my way around the table our eyes met again and we booth giggled at each other. "Hello" I said as I reached out my hand for hers, "my name is Amber. What's yours?"

Slowly, she grabbed my hand and shook it. "I'm Alexis. Nice to meet you Amber."

I quickly looked around to see if she was here with anyone, but it didn't appear to me that she was. "Are you here by yourself?" I asked cautiously.

A look of embarrassment fleeted across her face. Softly she whispered, "Yes, I am."

I put on the biggest smile I could muster and replied, "So am I! Would you like to enjoy the festival together?" As I looked at her, I saw the wheels in her head turning. Was I about to embarrass myself?

Luckily, she smiled and said, "Sure, why not? Let's give it a shot." I let out a sigh of relieve.

Come to think of it, we ended up hitting it off big time and we had so much in common. We spent three hours together at the festival that day just shopping, eating, and running our mouths. She was such a sweet young woman who had moved here two years ago from Manning, SC by herself. Alexis was twenty-four years old, and wise beyond her years. She was one of those young women who had their life mapped out and was doing everything within her power to make those things a reality. I could tell that she was one of those people who could help me grow as a person; I definitely needed to keep in contact with her. Before we left the festival that night, we ended up exchanging numbers and promised to call each other the next day.

To my surprise, Alexis turned out to be a major blessing in my life. She was the big sister that I never had, but always wanted. We spent so much time together that people started thinking that we were conjoined at the hip. Being around her really started changing my general view on life and she filled my whole life with so much positivity. Those positive vibes had me so engulfed that April and I started drifting apart. The crazy thing is, I wasn't even attracted to Alexis in that way. This was a budding friendship that I knew would be lifelong.

Over the next three months business was still booming. All services where full price and all of my staff had built a strong customer base. We were doing very well for a newer black owned hair salon. One of my rules for the salon was no personal drama. I made sure that all of my staff adhered by it and placed a sign in the window so that customers knew that that type of behavior was not allowed in my salon.

As I sat at the front counter while greeting customers, I saw April through the glass window. I was surprised to see her since we hadn't spoken in a week. She was wearing a teal and white stripped knee length dress with some teal wedges. As she walked through the door and saw me, a cool smile spread across her beautiful face. As she embraced me, she asked if she could speak to me in private.

Oh no! I thought to myself. I hope I didn't do anything wrong this time. I obliged to her request and led the way straight to my office.

Upon her closing the door to my office, she turned around and faced me with a look on her face that I had never seen before. What the hell was going on? I thought to myself.

"Is everything alright with you my love?" I asked her gently as I walked up to her to embrace her. As I reached my arms out to her, she backed up away from me and leaned her back against the door. I stopped dead in my tracks and stared at her with confusion. "April?"

All of a sudden, a chill ran down my spine as the entire vibe in the atmosphere changed.

"You know what Amber; I can't do this anymore. I thought you and I were going to be the perfect lesbian couple, but we're not. Fucking you is cool and all, but I miss my big black cocks. I don't think I'm cut out for this lesbian shit 24/7. I'm more of a once every blue moon type lesbian. I'm sorry for leading you and making you believe that this was something that it's not. I've been cheating on you for the past month and I've felt so bad about it. I know this is an inconvenient and inappropriate time, but I wanted to get this over with. Before you ask, no we can't be friends, I don't want anything else to do with you. I wish you nothing but success though."

With that she turned to open the door. I rushed to grab her hand as tears began descending down my face. "April, please don't do this!" I said just as I grabbed her right hand.

She yanked her hand away from mine as she turned and took one last look at me. Her facial expression was stoned, but I could see the tears welling up in her eyes. As she stared at me, her lips began to quiver as she said, "Amber, it's over." With that, she walked out of my life forever.

I spent the rest of that day wallowing in sadness. It was so hard to the point where I stayed holed up in my office all day with the door locked. I didn't understand what had transpired in my office. How did it get to that point? It had only been a week since we hadn't spoken to each other. She seemed so happy and in love, I couldn't even tell that something was majorly wrong or off between us. We had just made love a week ago and she told me how much she adored and loved me. Yet she admitted that she was cheating on me for a month. I know things had gotten a little different since I started hanging out with Alexis, but it wasn't that different. My first breakup ever and I'm a complete mess.

One of my client's husband came into the salon and going off on her for cheating on him while I wallowed in self-pity in my office. The commotion was so loud that I had no choice, but to pull myself together and go handle the situation, considering the fact I still had a business to run. I had to nip that in the bud quickly by putting him out. The last thing I wanted was negative press associated with my name or Hairlicious Designz. I was trying to take this salon as far as I possibly could. Last week the local news had done a piece on Hairlicious Designz, so it was free advertising for the salon. It was so humbling being able to see myself on the television. In a few more months, I would have made back all the money that I invested into this business.

7 FUCKING LIFE

As a rule of thumb of mine I would always be the one to close the salon down at night. This particular night, Jamie who left me in the salon alone, had forgotten to lock the door behind herself. I heard the doorknob jingle, so I swiftly turned around praying that it was just Jamie having forgotten something. Boy was I wrong.

A scream left my lips as soon as I realized who it was. "What's wrong beautiful?" he said in that creepy distant tone that he would use sometimes. I immediately started backing away from this monster. Slowly, he began walking toward me with this sinister scowl on his face. Damn it Jamie, I thought to myself. Why didn't you lock the fucking door? I never wanted to see this crazy motherfucker ever again.

I let out a deep breath as I said, "Uncle Samuel please…. what are you doing here?"

He laughed demonically as he attempted to mock me. "You know what the fuck I came here for bitch. Where's my fucking money?" he said angrily.

Slowly, I started shaking my head as I backed away from him. In the calmest voice I could muster I looked Uncle Samuel dead in his eyes and said, "I don't know what the fuck you're talking about Uncle Samuel. I don't have your money."

Uncle Samuel dashed toward me screaming, "You stole my money and ran away from the house you thieving little bitch. I'm going to kill you."

Just as he raised his hand to strike me Keitha, one of the braiders, walked in. She was so caught up in her phone that she wasn't even paying attention when she walked in. "Keitha!" I yelled louder than I should have."

Reluctantly she looked up from her phone. "Hey Amber, I'm so glad I caught you while you were still here. I forgot my damn phone charger. Who's your friend?" She said licking her lips seductively at Uncle Samuel. This bitch was dumber than a bird flying into a glass window. Did she not notice anything suspicious? Could she not see the fear that engulfed my face?

Uncle Samuel quickly adjusted his body language. That deceiving smile crossed his face as he stepped up and reached out his hand to Keitha. "Hello beautiful" he said in a voice that would make an ordinary woman swoon. "My name is Samuel. I'm Amber's uncle." Slowly he brought Keitha's hand to his mouth and kissed it gently.

Disgust ran through my body as this bitch began blushing. As his mouth lingered on her hand she giggled and said, "Nice to meet you Samuel. I'm Keitha, one of Amber's braiders for the salon. I just came to get my phone charger; I'll grab it and give you two some privacy."

As Keitha walked off to her station Uncle Samuel turned that menacing gaze toward me and mouthed "It's not over yet bitch."

I quickly grabbed my purse and keys and headed to the door just as Keitha was heading back. Uncle Samuel stepped in my path cutting me off.

"Keitha, I'm going to walk out with you girl." I said frantically. Loudly I said, "Uncle Samuel it was good catching up with you, I hope you have a safe trip back. I need to talk to Keitha about something." Stepping around him I walked out of the door with Keitha and we stood there waiting on him to follow. The anger was evident on his face as he walked out of the salon and walked off into the darkness. Quickly, I locked the salon door, ran to my car and locked the car doors. Keitha stood there confused as I pulled off without saying a word.

As I drove home, I didn't even realize that I was crying until a tear fell on my bare arm. What the hell was Uncle Samuel talking about? I didn't steal any money from him. Ted, the man he slutted my body out to had given me that money for my birthday. It was his way of penance for raping me. There was no way in hell I would steal from Uncle Samuel. The only accusation that I was guilty of was running away. I had no choice; Uncle Samuel was and still is a horrible person.

Pulling up to my apartment, I looked around to make sure I wasn't being followed. The coast seemed clear, so I gathered my belongings, pulled out my house key, and ran to my front door. I quickly unlocked the house door and rushed inside. I made sure to lock and bolt the door very well before I let out the breath that I was holding. Uncle Samuel is a very dangerous man, I have to protect myself from him. If he thinks I stole his money, he's not going to go away easily this time. The last thought that crossed my mind when I laid down that night was to survive at whatever cost.

The next day, I woke up and decided not to go to the salon. I need to survive I thought to myself. As 9:30 am rolled around, I got dressed and was walking out of the house at 10:00 am. Twenty minutes later I was pulling into the gun shop. I was going to protect myself from that maniac.

The guy at the gun shop was so nice and attentive. He went through the different types of gun with me and gave me his input on which gun would be the best for a female beginner like me. Walking out of the store I felt very confident with my brand-new black Glock 19. Fifteen minutes later I was sitting at the firing range getting a safety briefing on how to properly handle my weapon inside the range. Being that I never shot a gun before, I was the most attentive person in the class. The instructor was very knowledgeable and didn't make me feel dumb for asking any questions.

Four hours later, I walked out of the range feeling more comfortable than ever with my weapon. I was ready for this bastard if he wanted to try me again. I was so lost in my thought that I didn't realize that I had made it home. As I opened the car door, I heard someone shout my name. My body automatically went into panic mode and I reached out for my gun container.

"Amber?" the voice repeated.

I looked over to see Alexis sitting in the car that was next to me. I exhaled to let the fear escape from my body.

"Hey Alexis, how are you? You scared the living daylights out of me!" I said with a nervous giggle.

"I am so sorry. I didn't mean to scare you, Amber. I just left Tony's Grill and figured I'd stop by since I was in the area. Are you okay?" She asked showing genuine concern about me.

I quickly wiped the bead of sweat away that had formed on my brow, "Yeah girl, I'm good. Come on up."

I stood there debating on whether or not I should let her see the gun that I had just purchased. Not being one to fare well with being questioned, I then opted to leave the gun in the car and retrieve it once she was gone. Inside, my stomach was in a knot and my thoughts where focused solely on that fear I felt just a few minutes prior. The way the fear overcame me was truly overwhelming. Would I really be able to defend myself against Uncle Samuel? The fear that he had instilled in me when I lived with him was still in my heart. Although I purchased this gun, it wouldn't be able to protect me unless I had the courage to make use of it. Could I really shoot someone?

"Amber? Are you alright?" Alexis asked gently, interrupting my thoughts.

Quickly, I snapped out of it. "Yes, I'm fine. I was just thinking about what all I need to get done this week." I said as I headed toward the house.

Once we went inside, I poured us each a glass of lemonade and we lounged on the couch. As I looked at Alexis sitting on the couch, she looked troubled. Everything in my gut was telling me we were about to have a heart to heart.

"Alexis" is everything ok? You look troubled." I said gently. Slowly, she turned her eyes upon me and stared at me for a few seconds.

"You know Amber, sometimes, I worry so much about you."

I was so dumbfounded by her statement that I stuttered, "Wh-what why? I'm doing alright, don't worry about me." The sadness that filled her eyes when she looked at me brought tears to my eyes.

"The fear that you had on your face earlier when I called your name, it took me back to my childhood. A period of time in my life when my father use to touch me inappropriately. For years whenever someone would sneak up on me unannounced, I would get that same look on my face. The fear would be so great that it would paralyze me. Excuse me for being blunt, but were you taken advantage of sexually in your life? I noticed that you never talk about your old life?" She said cautiously.

As I sat there staring at her, emotions flooded my body as I thought about what she had just said to me. She was raped as a child and I would have never guessed. Her life is so put together, like nothing like that had ever happened to her. How did she manage to break free of those demons? I wonder if they haunted her as much as they haunted me. How did she get rid of that burden? Tears welled up in my eyes, as lies slipped through my pursed lips.

"Oh Alexis, I'm so sorry that you had to go through that. Some people can be so wretched. The world is filled with so much evil; for the last few years I've been so disappointed with mankind. I've never had to deal with anyone putting their hands on me though. However, I must ask, how did you put all of that behind you and move on with your life?" I asked curiously.

As I watched Alexis her face was a mixture of pain, sadness, and some emotions that I couldn't quiet place my finger on. After a few minutes of silence, I thought that she wasn't going to answer me. However, just as I opened my mouth to break the silence that had settled in, I heard a voice that I didn't recognize. Looking around confused, my gaze landed back on Alexis as I noticed her mouth moving. I had never heard her talk in this melancholy tone before.

"You know Amber," she said "that is a wonderful question. For years my father would take me on father daughter trips to various cities where he would molest me. After each time he would threaten to kill my mother and I if I ever told anyone. It started to take an emotional toll on me and left me a shell of a person. It was to the point where I stopped talking to people. I let my bonds with my friends break until they disappeared, my grades started dropping in school until I was failing every subject, and I spent all of my time holed up in my room. I had given up on life and it showed.

One night my mother came into my room, sat in the chair across from my bed, and just stared at me. We sat there staring at each for thirty minutes not saying a word, we were just there in each other's presence. All of a sudden, a tear ran down my mother's face, followed by a constant flow of huge pear-shaped tears. The presence that filled that room as I watched my mom sit there broken and defeated was suffocating to me. I couldn't breathe as images of my father raping me started flashing before my eyes. As the images became too much, the tear dam opened up and tears streamed down my face.

Before I knew it, my mother jumped up from that chair and was sitting beside me, hugging me to her bosom. She told me that no matter what issue I was having or whatever problem I was facing, she would be right there beside me to fight the demons that were haunting me. At that moment, I felt that motherly love ooze out from her skin and engulf me. It was at that moment that I found my voice again.

I started from the beginning and told my mother everything. The pain that crossed her face almost made me stop talking again, but she encouraged me to continue. After I told her everything, she told me that she couldn't take away what had happened to me, but she could prevent it from happening again. She walked to the phone on my computer desk and called 911. Twelve minutes later the police knocked on the front door. My body tensed up as an eerie feeling came across me. My mother didn't let go of her embrace around me as we sat on my bed waiting for the next knock on the front door. Just as the next knock landed, we heard my dad open the front door.

As soon as we heard the person at the door state their occupation and their name, my mother grabbed my hand and pulled me up as we headed towards the living room. I swear what happened next felt like we were living in the Twilight Zone. When we walked into the living room, my mother announced our presence to the officers. The moment my father heard my mother's voice he bellowed "What the hell is going on Ruby?" As the word Ruby left his mouth, he turned around expecting to just see my mother. As his brain registered the scene playing out in front of him, his eyes landed on me. The anger and malice could be heard in his voice as he yelled, "A-lex-is, you little snitching bitch. Didn't I tell you that if you ever told your mother I would…" I guess he realized what he was about to say because he stopped.

The officers stepped inside the house and told everyone to take a seat while they got everything sorted out. In the five seconds that the officers took their gaze off of us, dad had reached into the drawer near him and pulled out a knife. He was running towards us and my mother left out a scream to get the officers attention. As they turned around, they quickly pulled out their gun and yelled, "Sir Stop, please put down the weapon."

The gap between my father and us was getting smaller. The officers yelled one more time at my father to stop but he didn't stop. All I heard was a pop, pop, pop, agggggghhhhhhhhh, and a loud thud as glass began to shatter. I quickly blinked my eyes a few times trying to get the scene that I witnessed from in front of me. All I saw was my dad laying through the glass of the coffee table and bright red blood surrounding him. A heart wrenching scream left my mouth just before I blacked out.

Needless to say, we didn't go to his funeral. After that day, I started going to see a psychologist. Dr. Nelson opened up my eyes and helped me cleanse my heart in the two years that I saw her. The biggest takeaway was to not blame myself; the situation wasn't my fault. The last principal that I learned with her was forgiveness. Not only did I have to forgive myself, but I had to forgive my dad too. After I was able to get to the point in my life where I was able to forgive my dad, I felt free and as if I could finally grow as a person. So, in a nutshell, that's how I became able to deal with my pain from the past." She said with a smile.

Ever since we met, something has always drawn me closer to Alexis. At this very moment, it hit me. It's her kindred spirit and her kind heart. She is a nurturer and a really good mentor. I was so blessed to have her in my life. What a blessing she was.

We spent the remainder of the evening laughing and talking and cleansing our minds of the problems in our lives. I always felt at peace when she was around, too bad I couldn't get the courage to tell her how my life was before she met me. Around 10:00 pm we called it a night and ended our girls night.

The next morning, I received a call at 8:00 am that woke me out of my sleep. Slowly rubbing the sleep out of my eyes, I glanced at the phone and saw that it was Keitha calling. What the hell, I thought to myself? Keitha never calls me, it must be important. Within ten seconds of answering the phone, I knew that today was not the day.

When I answered the phone, all Keitha said was, "Boss lady, come down to the shop ASAP. I'll explain when you get here." The silence after she hung up was deafening. When I knocked myself out of my daze, I quickly jumped out of the bed, got dressed, and headed to the salon as fast I could manage.

Pulling up to the salon, I saw nothing out of the ordinary except for the fact that there was a blue Chevy caprice parked in the farthest slot in the parking lot. As I pulled into my designated slot, I saw my stylists all huddled around watching my every move. Immediately upon exiting the car I yelled, "What the hell is going on here?"

They all looked at me sadly. My heart dropped and I felt like I couldn't breathe. They all nodded toward the salon as Keitha told me to go in.

Everything in my being told me not to go into that salon, but I called bullshit. Upon stepping up to the back door, I saw shattered glass littered across the ground. A fucking break in, I thought to myself. As I stepped on the broken glass leading through the salon threshold, my heart stopped beating at the ugly sight in front of me. Looking around, I began to cry brokenheartedly. Big, fat, ugly tears cascaded down my face. Just then the room started spinning and I felt myself falling as my eyes rolled back into my head.

When I came back to my normal self, I remembered what caused me to faint. Slowly, I stood up and starting walking around the shop trying to see all of the damage that had been done. Shampoo and conditioner bottles were strewed across the floor. Whoever did this had time to pour all of the contents of the bottles on the floor and spread them across the mirrors and chairs. Each chair had been slashed prior to the shampoo and conditioner being poured on them. The stench of relaxers hit my nose the farther I walked into the shop. Looking at the mirrors closer to the front of the store, I saw relaxer smeared across the mirrors that weren't cracked.

I looked around and saw the pity in all of their eyes. Disappointment and anger began to battle inside of me trying to determine who would win. My first thought was to call the cops, but the last thing I wanted to do was to have the cops poking around in my life. I went to the back and grabbed a trash bag and started cleaning up the mess without saying a word. stylists followed suit and helped me to clean every inch of the shop. Just as we placed towels over the sliced-up cushions of the stylist chairs, our first customer for the day walked in. I quickly explained what happened and apologized for the mess. Luckily for me, all of the customers were sympathetic about it, and donated money to help me get the shop repaired. That was the longest day of my life, but I made it through.

    That night as I left the shop, I had an eerie feeling throughout my body that would not go away. Today had been the longest day of my life. Deep down in my heart, I knew for sure that Uncle Samuel was the culprit behind everything that happened at the shop. Not only was he threatening my life, but he had messed with my money also. That is where I have to draw the line, I thought to myself. I could not believe that he had the audacity to destroy my shop like that. What he did was fucked up and totally unacceptable by me.

8 UNCLE "FUCKING" SAMUEL

Driving through town, I was so focused on sorting out my thoughts that I didn't pay attention to my surroundings. My mind was on autopilot as I drove to my favorite spot to see the live oaks draped with Spanish moss. It wasn't until I had placed the car in park and climbed onto my hood with my blanket that I heard a car approaching. Quickly, I ran back inside the car and grabbed my gun. Tucking it away underneath the blanket I climbed back on the hood of my car and sat there as terror engulfed my entire body. This was a hidden spot by Wormsloe State Historic site, so no one should be out here at this hour. A few seconds later the car pulled up about 10 feet far away from me. Their lights turned off and I heard the door open. Slowly, I looked over and my heart fell out of my chest. There was the car that was parked in the salon parking lot this morning when I got to work.

As my eyes continued scanning the scene before me, my eyes landed on Uncle Samuel in the flesh. The demonic smile that covered his face ran a chill down my spine. He must have followed me all the way from the salon. Quickly, I racked my brain trying to remember if anyone was in the car when I left work. I was so focused internally, that I didn't think anything of the car when I saw it again. Fuck, I thought to myself. He slowly started approaching me.

"Don't come any closer Uncle Samuel!" I yelled as I climbed off the hood of the car, still holding my loaded gun in the blanket as my defense. I'm so thankful that this place had a few lamp posts, so the area wasn't covered in complete darkness.

The smile immediately left his face as he began yelling, "Listen here you dirty little thieving slut, you better give me my motherfucking money bitch!"

"Uncle Samuel, I mean daddy, I didn't steal any money from you. Ted gave me a bag full of money for my birthday. He apologized to me and told me to use the money to escape and start my life anew." I saw Uncle Samuels shoulders swell with anger.

Spit began flying out from his mouth as his speech and actions became more belligerent. "Don't try that daddy shit on me hoe! I will fucking kill you if you don't give me back my money Amber" he shouted angrily.

Without hesitation, I dropped the blanket onto the ground and held out my Glock 19 and pointed it directly at his center mass.

He took a step back as the gun startled him. "What the fuck Amber, are you going to kill your old man? If you shoot me and don't kill me, I will murder your stupid and ungrateful black ass. Unless you intend on using that, you better put the gun down lil' bitch."

Slowly, he started progressing toward me again. "Stop right there or I'll shoot you dead Uncle Samuel! I don't want to do this! Just leave me alone! I keep telling you I didn't take your money. If someone stole your money, it wasn't me. Your beef isn't with me!"

My pleas fell on deaf ears. Uncle Samuel continued to walk toward me with that evil look in his eyes like he was going to tear me apart if he got hold of me. Was this the final show down? Everything in my soul was telling me that one of us wasn't leaving this historical site alive tonight. I had no intentions of my life ending this soon, so I stubbornly stood my ground. I shouted one more plea for him to leave me alone, but he didn't heed my warning. I quickly fired a warning shot in the air, but he ignored it and continued advancing toward me.

"Damn it Uncle Samuel!" I yelled sadly. Without hesitation I pulled the trigger as he continued advancing towards me. A look of confusion crossed Uncle Samuel's face as he looked down and saw bright red blood streaming out from his chest, saturating his once white shirt. Covering the bullet hole with his right hand, he slowly raised his head and stared at me with more dreadful anger.

This was definitely one of those moments where if looks could kill, he would have murdered me. The cold look in his eyes as he started stumbling toward me let me know that his words earlier were true. I had to kill him, or he was going to kill me. Visions of the hell that he had put me through began playing before my eyes like a movie. Rape, abuse, sexual exploitation, invasion of privacy, and the list continued. How could a father do this to his only child? The anger that was welled up inside of me finally exploded. Uncle Samuel took another step toward me and I snapped.

"Fuck you Uncle Samuel!" I yelled as I emptied the clip into him.

The scream that left his mouth sent a chill down my spine. It looked like he was having a seizure as his bloodied body fell to the ground in a clump and started convulsing. Tears began pouring down my face as I realized that he was dead and gone, my nightmare was finally over. I could finally breathe easy again. As I sat there in the dirt crying, I realized that I had nothing whatsoever to cry about. This man made my life a living hell, and he was not worth my tears at all.

Composing myself, I decided to take any money that he had on his person and in his car. Taking a paper towel out of my car, I quickly searched him and the car, making sure not to leave any fingerprints. After completing my search, I got into my car and drove away. On my way home, I stopped by the Savannah River, cleaned my gun, and threw it into the river. Hopefully getting rid of the evidence forever.

Twenty minutes later, I was walking into the house. As soon as I closed and locked the front door, my body collapsed to the ground as tears and sobs overtook it. I couldn't believe I had killed another man. I am officially a murderer. That night, I ended up crying myself to sleep.

The next few days I ended up holing myself up in my apartment. I didn't go to work, didn't answer or return phone calls, didn't eat; I was just consumed by the darkness of all that I had been through. Depression kicked in heavily and I found myself contemplating my life over the next five days. It was to the point where I just couldn't take the voices of the men I had killed screaming inside of my head. I hadn't eaten for days and I was all out of tears. As I laid in my bed, I remembered that I saw a guy selling drugs on the corner by the corner store. I threw on some gray Nike sweats and a matching hoodie, washed my face, and walked to my car.

Five minutes later, I pulled up and parked across the street from the corner store. I sat there watching the dope man posted up on the corner. Within a few seconds he had scanned the area and our eyes connected with each other. I smiled at him and got out of the car. Nervously, I made my way toward him.

Amber, what the fuck are you doing? I thought to myself. You are not about to possibly go through with buying drugs from this dope man. You are a successful black business owner and you already have so much going for you. What if this drug is a gate way to something else, what if you become addicted, or what if you overdose on this? Pull yourself out of this darkness baby girl.

Instead of listening to the voice in my head, I ignored it. "Hey Sexy, how are you?" I said with a smile.

He eyed me cautiously as he said, "Are you 5-0?"

I looked him dead in his eyes as I told him, "Fuck no! I'm just a bitch trying to take the pain away."

He eyed me up and down once more, and then calmly said, "What can I do for you miss?"

Looking around nervously, I leaned in and whispered, "Do you have any oxycodone?"

He laughed as he said, "I have the 512's going five for $60."

I looked at him confused. "What the hell are 512's, I asked for oxycodone?"

I could see him getting annoyed as he said, "512's is what you want shorty?"

Reluctantly, I pulled out $60 and gave it to him. He reached out to shake my hand as he slid the bag in my hand. I thanked him and quickly scurried away.

The entire trip home, I contemplated whether or not I was going to take those 512's. A quick Google search revealed that 512's was actually one of the street names for oxycodone. At least ole dude wasn't trying to get over on me. By the time I made it into the house, I had made up my mind. Fuck this life, I thought to myself. At that moment my phone began to ring. Looking at it, I saw that it was you calling. Well doesn't she have the perfect timing, I thought to myself as I let the phone go to voice mail.

Walking into the kitchen, I fixed myself a glass of Hennessey and popped all five pills. Singing and sashaying down the hall, I slowly made my way to my bedroom. Just as I went to climb on the bed, I blacked out.

Now, here we are Alexis.

Alexis was just staring at me speechless. Tears were running down her face as she got up and gave me the biggest hug. She said a quick prayer for my health, mental state, and wellbeing.

As she began wiping away her tears she said, "Amber, you are such a strong woman. I admire and look up to you. I just want you to know that I promise not to ever leave your side. We are going to get this sis. I'm going to take care of you and get you to the next healthy phase in your life!"

I could hear the sincerity in her voice as I smiled up at her. She is something special and I need her in my life. As she sat next to me on the hospital bed, a sense of relief washed over me. Finally, being able to tell someone my story made me feel like I could breathe again.

    I leaned over and kissed Alexis smack dab on her lips. She blushed, and then leaned in to kiss me back. The love pouring from her body engulfed me entirely and it reassured me that everything was going to be alright. I had a long recovery ahead of me, but with Alexis by my side, I'm sure that I can overcome any obstacle that is thrown my way.

ABOUT THE AUTHOR

KALA JANAE was born in Manning, SC. and raised in the small town of Tyler, TX. She spent eleven years in the United States Air Force, where she was able to travel and defend our freedom. For many years, she was enticed by the likes of Zane and Eric Jerome Dickey. Kala made a promise to herself to be like them one day. She uses life experiences mixed with fiction to take the reader on an adventure that they won't forget.

Made in the USA
Coppell, TX
09 September 2021